Made by Sea and W...
strange and highly origin...
shadowy margins of an immigrant fishing community, it is
sometimes brutal, sometimes funny, sometimes poignant—
sometimes all of these things and more. This is a beautiful and
disturbing novel in stories which deserves a wide readership.

Jonathan Taylor, author of *Entertaining Strangers* and *Melissa*

Made by Sea and Wood, in Darkness is a collage of many
lives and many voices, based around an all-night café in a
Greek port. Funny and subversive, sometimes heartbreaking,
this is writing from the edge that pushes at the boundaries of
contemporary fiction.

Ailsa Cox, author of *Writing Short Stories*

The reader of the linked stories that comprise *Made by Sea
and Wood, in Darkness* is transported to the all-night Café
Papaya in the Greek seaport of Kavala, a scruffy hangout for
weathered Egyptian fishermen and ragged locals. Servers at
the café, Pavlo and Angie feel alienated from this brutish world
of raunchy, wretched men. Evoking that world, Alexandros
Plasatis, who was born in Greece but lives in England, is in full
command of his adopted English. Like one of his misplaced
Egyptians, Plasatis makes his words 'sound like breaking
crackers.'

Steven G. Kellman,
author of *The Translingual Imagination* and *Redemption*

In this startling collection, a novel in stories, Alexandros Plasatis
explores the lives, loves and tales of Egyptian fishermen in
Greece. Funny, filthy, unsettling, and often unexpectedly
moving, these tales from the margins are beautifully crafted,
and mark the arrival of a distinctive new voice in fiction.

Will Buckingham, author of *The Descent of the Lyre*

Made By Sea And Wood, In Darkness

a novel in stories

Alexandros Plasatis

SPUYTEN DUYVIL
NEW YORK CITY

Library of Congress Cataloging-in-Publication Data

Names: Plasatis, Alexandros, author.
Title: Made by sea and wood, in darkness : a novel in stories / Alexandros
Plasatis.
Description: New York City : Spuyten Duyvil, [2021] |
Identifiers: LCCN 2021001012 | ISBN 9781952419522 (paperback)
Subjects: LCSH: Immigrants--Fiction. | Egyptians--Greece--Fiction.
Classification: LCC PR6116.L37 M33 2021 | DDC 823/.914--dc23
LC record available at https://lccn.loc.gov/2021001012

Jonathan Taylor opened a door when no-one else would. Neil Taylor described the English words of the unwanted. X taught me the words of the Arabs. Sterios stood by me.

Versions of the following stories have been previously published in Unthology, Crystal Voices: Ten Years of Crystal Clear Creators, blÆkk: An Anthology of Short Stories and Illustrations, Adelaide: Independent Quarterly Literary Magazine, Meat for Tea: The Valley Review, Meridian: The Semiannual from the University of Virginia, Bull: Men's Fiction, Aji Magazine, Phenomenal Literature: A Global Journal Devoted to Language and Literature, Whistling Shade: Literary Journal, Qwerty, The Main Street Rag, The Los Angeles Review of Los Angeles, Another Chicago Magazine and J Journal: New Writing on Justice.

For Sotiris, who taught me everything

Either you are a writer or you are not. If you're a writer for a specific nation or a specific race, then fuck you.
Dambudzo Marechera

Contents

THE LEGEND OF ZARAMAROUQ

1

Pavlo began working in Café Papaya the summer he turned fourteen. Morning shifts. The terrace was big and busy. He learnt quickly, served quickly, and liked it busy. The customers were difficult. Too much froth in their coffee, not enough ice-cubes in their pop, pigeon droppings on the seats, ants crawling up the trees, leaves falling from the trees, flies, hot hot hot, oh too hot, ah yeah, ah they liked the trees' shadows, ah nice, ah so nice, the sun moved, oh no, they had to move into the shade again. Some made jokes, but they made the same jokes every day. Some were all right, some were good, and Zaramarouq was Egyptian.

Pavlo didn't know that Zaramarouq was Egyptian. He didn't care what he was. He only admired him. Zaramarouq usually came to the café at around 11am with three or four Greek fishermen, who were all around thirty-five or forty. It was really busy at 11am, coffees coffees coffees, but every time Pavlo went to take Zaramarouq's order, suddenly everything would hush. So strange how everything hushed. Zaramarouq would give a simple greeting to Pavlo, like, 'What's up, Pavlo? How's everything? HAHA!' Pavlo liked the way Zaramarouq spoke, because he liked simple things and because his voice was strong and crisp. His accent made some words sound like breaking crackers, a tasty accent. He thought that his laughter was a giant's laughter. In Pavlo's eyes, Zaramarouq was a giant, wind-beaten and sea-beaten with deep wrinkles. They looked good, the deep wrinkles. Huge and solid arms and thighs he had. And broad shoulders and enormous fists with great big knuckles, and fingers full of net-cuts, and brown, wild hair, thick-like-needles hair, hair in all directions, mad hair. This strange giant always ordered his frappé pulling ridiculous faces—imitating someone who strains to shit, an orgasmic woman, a sobbing boy, stuff like that—never failing to make Pavlo giggle.

When one of his companions behaved like the other customers and dared to complain to Pavlo about a coffee or something, Zaramarouq would cut them short: 'Shut up, you moaning arsehole! You got your period again?' His companions laughed at these quips, but their eyes betrayed discomfort and even fear. Without a care, Zaramarouq would laugh his giant laughter and turn to Pavlo: 'Take your time, Pavlo, bring us the coffee whenever you feel like it.' Pavlo, balancing on one hand a tray full of pop and coffees, would say nothing, he would only laugh with his big friend, making sure he didn't spill the drinks. And when he realised that the customers became impatient with him just standing there and looking at Zaramarouq, he would go back to serving quickly. So the hours and the days in the café would pass quickly, until the next time Zaramarouq would come to hold the morning back.

Something else that hushed the café's terrace was when Zaramarouq told dirty stories to his companions. Pavlo couldn't get enough of these. The young waiter worked out a system so as not to appear that he was slacking: when serving, he always tried to walk past Zaramarouq, and if he heard him telling one of his tales, he would go to a nearby table with his cloth and give it a wipe down, then the backs of the chairs and the legs of the chairs, listening and stealing glances at the storyteller who stirred his imagination:

'…and she sits exactly opposite me. EXACTLY opposite. And she opens her legs! Like THIS!' Zaramarouq opened his legs, pulled aside his shorts with one hand, 'and she does THIS!' he brushed the fingers up and down near his genitals: 'Like this, like this… And she flashes at me her cunt-lips!' and, knowing that the young waiter was watching him, he would catch Pavlo's eye and pull a face: 'Un-fucking-believable'—then get on with the story.

And so, the waitering mornings continued on in that way, busy and giggly and dirty, until the day Zaramarouq got into a fight.

It was 2.30pm, the shift was going to finish soon and Pavlo was sitting by the bar, waiting for the time to pass. The terrace was almost empty. Zaramarouq and his companions, two Greek fishermen in their fifties, were sitting at the far corner and had been served. Served also was a group of four Greek fishermen who were sitting not far from the bar. Zaho Castrioti was one of them. Pavlo didn't like Zaho Castrioti. Zaho had short blond hair, he was getting bald, and was the same age as Zaramarouq and maybe as big as him. But he always seemed annoyed about something and Pavlo was a bit scared of him.

Two or three tables away from Zaho's group, two couples of foreign tourists settled down, well-dressed and well-groomed, the sort that didn't come often to Café Papaya. They seemed to be travellers on their way to the opposite island, Thassos, and as they were waiting for the ferry, they had decided to have a break and freshen up.

'Hi. What would you like, please?'

Two frappes, two fresh orange juices.

Served.

Pavlo was glad that these blond travellers stopped at the café where he was working. From here, they could see so many nice things. The fishermen who were scattered all along the harbourside, sitting cross-legged in front of the caïques, mending nets. They could see the hill with the Old Town, its fort and walls and aqueduct, the roofs of the Imaret—left behind by Byzantines, Venetians, Ottomans. Lots of history. Maybe they liked history. Pavlo didn't know who built what, he would be embarrassed if they asked him, he hoped they didn't. The sky was blue and the sea was bluer and the island opposite was dark dark green. The blond travellers had all that to take in and they had good coffee to keep their eyes alert and nice thick shadows from the lemon trees to keep them cool.

That was what Pavlo was thinking, sitting on the barstool by himself, smiling to no-one, when an old man appeared. A tall, skinny, drunk old man with a fishermen's hat and a white beard that shimmered under the hot sun. Ah, this old man used to be a kind fisherman, Pavlo imagined, who had taught the wood of his boat to be friends with the sea. Pavlo imagined that the old man had weakened over the years and one day the sea-worm inside him died, and he turned to wine, and drank and drank to mix some red in all that blue.

Anyway. The old fisherman walked slowly between tables, grabbing onto the backs of chairs to keep steady. He took his time walking and finally stopped in front of Zaho Castrioti's table and muttered something.

Zaho ignored him and the old man stood there, looking at Zaho with his drunk old eyes. Zaho never looked at him, he only looked annoyed. The old man muttered again. Zaho, without looking at him, said, 'Go away.'

From the corner of the terrace, Zaramarouq's voice was heard: 'Leave the grandpa alone, you hear me?'

Zaho turned his head slowly and stared at Zaramarouq. Five seconds. He looked away.

The old man closed his eyes, he wiped spittle from his mouth and the hairs around it, and dried his palm on his trousers. He muttered away. Zaho looked straight ahead and took a deep breath and the old man kept on trying to tell him something, and Zaho snapped: 'GET THE HELL OUT OF HERE AND GO AND FUCK YOURSELF,' and all of a sudden Zaramarouq shot off like a cannonball towards Zaho Castrioti: 'I TOLD YOU TO LEAVE THE GRANDPA ALONE.' A heavy glass ashtray was hanging from Zaramarouq's fingers, it glistened as he was bull-running through the terrace, forcing his way straight ahead, no need to manoeuvre between tables: tables and chairs that stood in his way took a tumble, ashtrays twirled, menus shot away, everything making way for Zaramarouq to attack, everything half-frightened and half-excited to see him in action.

Zaho hadn't got time to move from his chair. Zaramarouq smashed the ashtray into Zaho's balding head and now the two giants charged each other, brow to brow, eye to eye, a mutual headlock.

Pavlo eyed-up Zaho's companions. They didn't move. He eyed-up Zaramarouq's companions. They didn't move. Eyed-up the travellers. They didn't move either.

Pavlo moved. He jumped up from his barstool and ran towards the giants. He didn't know what he would do once he got there, he just ran, and, when he got close enough, he took a leap and smashed a shoulder against Zaho's body.

He found himself on the floor, and the last thing he saw

before everything turned dark was Zaramarouq, kneeling over him, absorbing Zaho's boots and punches from behind.

When his vision returned, the tiles around him were sprayed with dried blood. He looked up. Zaramarouq wasn't there. Zaho's companions weren't there. The old man wasn't there. Pavlo thought that Zaho Castrioti wasn't there either, but then he saw Zaho on the floor, between tables and chairs. The two Greek fishermen in their fifties sliced open a cigarette and put wisps of tobacco on the cuts on his head, they poured water on his bloody face.

The young waiter got up. Got a broom and a shovel and brushed away broken glass and mugs and ashtrays. He put tables and chairs back up the right way, brought replacement ashtrays, wiped the menus clean and slid them under the ashtrays. Café Papaya looked all right again.

A police car pulled up in front of the café.

One of the fishermen helped Zaho away.

Two policemen took Pavlo to one side. Questions were asked, answers given: 'Yeah, there was a fight. No, don't really know them. A blond fisherman, bald really, and someone else. Um… It was the blond's fault.'

The other Greek fisherman approached. 'It was no-one's fault. The guys will sort it out between themselves.'

The policemen looked up at him.

'In a peaceful way,' the fisherman added.

The policemen left.

The fisherman left.

Only the blond travellers remained.

And Pavlo looked at the travellers, smiled at them. Then he went inside to wash the blood away. It wasn't his blood. He found a black t-shirt, took off his white, stained shirt, and changed it. When he came back out the travellers had gone. He took his tray and went over to clear their table. In between the empty cups and glasses, there was a small pile of coins. A tip.

A few days later, Pavlo heard that Zaho Castrioti had been coming down to the harbour every night, carrying a gun with him, searching all caïques, looking for Zaramarouq to kill. But Pavlo wasn't worried about Zaramarouq. Zaramarouq could beat up Zaho anytime, even if Zaho had a gun, because, for Pavlo, Zaramarouq was a legend.

Weeks passed by, months, and Zaramarouq came less and less to the café, until he stopped coming at all. Mid-September Pavlo went back to school and worked in Café Papaya for only a few hours on weekends. Sometimes, on Saturday afternoons, he saw Zaramarouq on his red motorbike, riding slowly in front of the café and turning his head to give a wave. Other times, when Pavlo strolled around the harbour, he saw Zaramarouq on a caïque, sitting cross-legged on a corner of the deck, working on the nets with his back against the town. His back was always turned against the town. 'Why is your back always turned against the town?' he wanted to ask, but didn't. Because he knew that Zaramarouq was a legend, and that's what legends do, they have their backs against whole towns, and hold a needle and a piece of net, and when they feel like it, they look up and gaze out to sea.

2

And as years passed by, Pavlo almost forgot about Zarama-rouq. He came to know other Egyptians, most of the hundred or so who worked on the caïques. The locals looked down on them, but Pavlo took a liking to these Egyptians, they were easy going and didn't moan or complain when the café was busy and he was slow to serve them. Word had spread in their community that when he was a boy he had defended the big Egyptian, and on his harbour strolls they would come over to talk with him, and he felt their admiration.

It was on one of these strolls, a hot afternoon down at the Port Authorities, where the fishermen were getting ready to go on their voyage, unloading ice from trucks into the caïques, that Pavlo heard Zaramarouq calling his name. The big man was leaning against a wooden pillar, half-hidden under the shadow of the wheel-house.

Pavlo stepped closer to the caïque.

Zaramarouq's voice cut him short: 'What you think about life in the harbour, Pavlo? You think it's like the old days?'

'I guess so,' Pavlo shouted. Pavlo had to shout. Zarama-rouq just spoke.

'No, it's not like the old days, Pavlo. And you know why? Because now the only thing everyone cares about is money. You got money? Everyone's your friend. No money? Go and fuck yourself.'

Now, this was how ordinary people talked, Pavlo thought. If it wasn't for Zaramarouq, he would say *yeah yeah*, just to get on with it. The world was full of ordinary people, but Zaramarouq was Zaramarouq, so Pavlo said, 'No, that's not what I think.'

'I can't hear you, Pavlo. What did you say?'

Pavlo shouted: 'That's not what I think. That's what *you* think.'

Zaramarouq stepped out of the shadow. He looked angry. But then, a small group of Egyptians approached Pavlo and cut Zaramarouq's step short. A group of Egyptians who had returned a few days ago from Ezbit El Burg and had presents for him, presents from Al Qaherah. They exchanged three kisses, Egyptian style, and Pavlo went on with his stroll, leaving Zaramarouq behind, feeling a bit of a legend himself.

3

Pavlo was a man when his old friend came to the café again. That was the first time he had seen Zaramarouq for years. He came with his wife, Soula. It was a late summer evening and Pavlo wasn't on duty, he was just hanging around. He liked just hanging around. The three of them sat at a table out on the terrace. Introductions were made. Then:

'But his name is Yiorgo Ahmoud. Don't tell me that you didn't know it? God, why didn't you tell him, Yiorgo? Of course, how would you know if no-one had told you? Zara-however you called him wasn't even his Egyptian name. That's no name at all, never heard it before. Yes, *Yiorgo* is the name he adopted when we got married. You didn't know he was married? Now now...'

Soula was Greek and Soula liked talking and so Soula talked: they had been married for twenty years; her husband came to Greece twenty-seven years ago; they would go back to Egypt sometimes for holidays; they had a son; their son was Pavlo's age; and then on and on and on.

Pavlo caught the attention of Angie the waitress. Nodded. She came over, flashed a smile. 'What can I get you guys?'

Soula and Zaramarouq wanted hot chocolate.

'And you, Pavlo?' Angie asked.

'Nah. I'm all right, cheers.'

Angie left.

Soula went on. 'Ah, yes, when I got married to Yiorgo…'

Zaramarouq hadn't changed much. Big and strong with mad hair and all. But he didn't talk a great deal, and, when he did talk, he seemed to be controlling his voice, trying to keep it down.

Hot chocolate was served.

'You sure you don't want anything, Pavlo?' Angie asked.

Yes, he was sure.

Soula kept on talking, Zaramarouq listening passively, Pavlo thinking about how much he had admired this man when he was a boy, and saying to himself that his only purpose at that table now, his *only* purpose, was to bring back the legend of Zaramarouq. But he shouldn't push things. He had to take it easy. Be patient.

Lighters were stroked, paper and tobacco burned, silver plumes of smoke rose in the dark cool evening, and Soula went on to talk about the big stories on the news those days, the wild behaviour of the tourists, especially those from Britain. The TV reported incidents of men going around dressed as women, nuns usually; of young females pulling up their tops and flashing their breasts to locals. Soula's cheeks turned pink as she talked, and she lowered her eyes down on her own breasts. She had large breasts. Pavlo looked at her breasts and Zaramarouq looked at her breasts and Soula saw them looking at her breasts. Then she asked why those foreign tourists behave like that. Neither Zaramarouq nor Pavlo answered, so Soula provided her own explanation:

'You see, these poor girls are away from home, that's why they do these things. They feel like doing something wild. Do you think *our* girls are any better? The other night—oh my God, Pavlo—we went with Yiorgo to this new beach-bar on the other side of town—have you ever been to that one, Pavlo?—and we were scandalised!'

Pavlo leaned forward. 'Oh yeah?'

'Yes, Pavlo. Hahaha. Goodness me!'

Pavlo kept his eyes on Soula: 'What happened in that beach-bar?'

'Well...' she re-adjusted her bum on the seat. 'We were sitting by a small table right on the sand and from the darkness near us, behind the rocks, we heard... we heard...' she paused and looked at her husband.

Pavlo sat back. Eyed Zaramarouq. He was looking at his wife, they were smiling at each other. Pavlo turned to Soula. 'So what did you hear from the darkness?'

'We heard: "Ah yes, yes, ah more, yes, yes, more..." Haha! My dear Pavlo, it was one girl and three men! *One* girl and *three* men. And the telly shows the English girls. Why? Are our girls any better? She took all three of them together, my dear Pavlo. Together. And she kept moaning. Haha...'

Pavlo and Zaramarouq laughed. Pavlo's laughter was stronger.

Soula sighed. Sipped her drink. Went on: 'Ah, Pavlo, Pavlo. Now you're in the best period of your life. Whatever you've got to do, you'll do it now. Once you grow up, forget everything. You'll get married and the wildest thing to do is come to Café Papaya and drink hot chocolate. You'll have kids, commitments. I got married and enslaved myself. What did I get out of it?'

'Oi! Bitch!' Zaramarouq snapped in such a loud and quirky voice that it made Pavlo sit back and laugh. 'Are you saying now that I don't take you out? It's you who wants to stay home. I keep telling you to go to places, but you don't like this, you don't like that–'

'No, my sweetheart, no. I'm not complaining. It's something else that I'm trying to say to Pavlo.'

Pavlo stubbed out his cigarette and had a good look at Soula. She was plump. Curvy plump. Jelly, bouncy, rubbery plump. He had noticed before that she had a nice, big round bum. Her skin was tanned and smooth and shiny, and her eyes big and green and almond-shaped. And as he kept staring at her, he saw those big green eyes giving a sidelong glance to her husband, he saw how her lips bent and formed a smile, how slowly those lips parted: 'If *they* come here, why don't *we* go to England?' Her cheeks turned pink again.

The couple looked at each other. She said: 'Would you take me there? Would you take me to London?'

'I would take you to London.' Then, to Pavlo. 'But I can't really take her to London. My passport has been seized.'

'How come?'

'Did some bullshit back in Egypt.'

'And your Greek passport?'

'Haven't got a Greek passport. They won't give me one.'

'Why not?'

'Because they keep playing with their little willies, that's why not.'

'Yes, Pavlo,' Soula said. 'After twenty-seven years here and married to a Greek, they won't give him a passport. Every year I've got to sign papers so that he won't be deported.'

'Bollocks to that,' said Pavlo.

'Exactly, Pavlo. Bollocks,' said Zaramarouq. 'If I wanted to, I could get Greek citizenship. I could have proper papers and everything. You know how many times they told me to go down to Athens and get a passport? But you know what else they said? They said that I'll have to get it through a window, Pavlo, not through the door. And I don't like getting in through windows. Me, Pavlo, if I ever get in, I'll get in through the door.'

Pavlo smiled. Zaramarouq didn't.

But Pavlo kept on smiling because he knew now that Zaramarouq was still a great man. He decided that now was the time to pull out the greatness of Zaramarouq, to turn him, once again, into a legend. He had no idea how he would do that. He only knew where to begin. They would talk about something that they had never talked about before, maybe that would help. But hot chocolate? A night like that, with stars and lemon trees and sea and legends and a cheerful woman, and they were having hot chocolate?

'I'll buy you a beer,' Pavlo said. 'Can I buy you a beer?'

The couple looked at each other. Smiled. 'Of course you can.'

Pavlo glanced at Angie. She was busy at the bar preparing an order. He went over and brought beers and glasses, and, while beers were poured and cigarettes lit, Pavlo looked at Zaramarouq and said, 'You remember when—'

'Yeah I remember,' said Zaramarouq. 'You want to talk about the fight with Zaho Castrioti, don't you?'

Pavlo and Zaramarouq had a few good gulps of beer. It was nice, cool beer, and they were warm inside.

Soula looked at them, had a sip.

Zaramarouq went on.

'Of course I remember.' He took a drag. 'HAHA!' It was a giant's *haha*. 'HA! I remember well.' More beer downed. 'You should stay out of these things. You could get hurt.' Plumes of smoke lingered around the table, and behind the silver smoke, Soula's big green eyes had something new as she looked at her husband who talked with passion. 'Did you see the others? No-one had moved.' Her eyes shot towards Pavlo. 'Yes, I remember that fight with the arsehole. But Zaho Castrioti was an arsehole and that's it. I remember that fight and I remember many more fights with other arseholes, but there's a fight I can't forget.'

'What fight?'

Zaramarouq put the glass down: 'The fight with Dino.'

'Ah!' Soula jumped up and clapped her hands. 'Ah yes yes! Dino! The fight with Dino!'

'You know Dino, the boxing champion?'

'Heard the name before.'

'Well,' said Zaramarouq. 'Listen now. I knew Dino and Dino knew me. He used to drink a lot at that period. He owned a tiny bar and his wife was the only barwoman. So one night I go to his bar and drink my whisky and Dino is already pissed. After a while he turns to me and says: "Oi! Leave my wife alone!" I say, "What're you talking about, Dino? I've done nothing." "You grabbed her arse! I SAW YOU GRABBING HER ARSE!" I tell him that I didn't grab her arse, but he's really angry. "You grabbed her arse, YOU DARK BAS-TARD." He leaps at me. I push him away. He throws a couple of punches, but it's easy to block him, he's drunk. 'You fake Muslim,' he says, 'you married a Christian, you drink alcohol, you changed your name, you fake Muslim.' Fake Muslim? I'm losing it. I hit him and he falls. I beat the shit out of him and leave him unconscious.

'One morning he finds me in the harbour and tells me to watch my step. He says nothing else.

'Some time passes and I go to another friend's tiny bar, again for a whisky. While I have my drink, I see Dino coming in, sober. I say to myself, "That's it. I must say my prayers now and fight the champion." That's what I said to myself, Pavlo. "How am I going to get through this one?"

'HA!

'He grabs a stool and smashes it against my face, and I fight blind. I feel the blows coming in quick and I can't breathe. I manage to get in two or three punches. When I regain my vision, I break his nose. He had me after that, he cornered me and turned my face into mince. Into MINCE he turned my face. I left the bar and my whole face was a wound. Mince and blood. Here, ask Soula. When I went home, she couldn't recognise me.'

Zaramarouq reached for his beer and finished it. 'Pavlo, Pavlo. I was beaten, Pavlo. Beaten.'

Pavlo caught the attention of Angie the waitress. Nodded.

Soula put her hand over her husband's hand. Her fingers ran through his great big knuckles.

Angie flashed a smile. 'What can I get you guys?'

'Beer,' said Zaramarouq.

IT WAS DAWN IN SALONICA, TOO

At around 2am Angie was sitting behind the open bar when a taxi stopped in front of Café Papaya. A guy stepped out, went straight to her, said, 'Pour me a *tsipouro* and pour one for yourself and come and sit down with me,' and, quickly turning around, he sat by a table in front of the bar's gazebo, next to the only other customers: two couples of around fifty who had just begun their meal of beef soup, Greek salad, tzatziki, and chilli cheese-cream.

Motionless, he gazed at the deserted harbour. His hair was short and grey, his lips fleshy, and he had small, grey eyes. Some long threads from the cut-off sleeves of his shirt dangled onto his strong tanned arms.

Angie filled three quarters of a small glass with *tsipouro* and a tall one with water and ice, put them on a small round tray, walked out of the bar, and served him: '*Stin iyia sas.*'

'Miss. Pour yourself one, too. On me. And come and sit down with me.'

'Thanks, but I'm working.'

Four customers arrived. Three lads, one girl. The guy remained motionless, except for his unblinking eyes that followed the young people as they walked under the lemon trees, in the middle of the large terrace, ten tables or so to his left. Once they took their seats, his eyes darted back to the harbour, his thick lips puckered, and he had his first sip of *tsipouro*.

Angie took their order. The guy had another sip.

When she returned to her bar, the guy half-turned and peered over his shoulder: 'Miss. Pour yourself a *tsipouro*.'

'I told you, I'm working.'

'I ask you to come over and keep me company and you say, "I'm working"? You've got no respect?'

'I've got respect. But I'm busy. When I'm not busy, I might join you.'

'Ah... Right. Let's see.'

He reverted to his previous state. Cross-legged, he moved his head slowly, scanning his surroundings, until finally he peeped to his right, at the married couples, and his lips puckered.

'Angieeee!' a female voice called out from within the café, and Angie got up and sauntered towards the source of the voice.

The guy smirked.

The waitress walked out holding three plates of spaghetti carbonara in her one hand and a tortellini in gypsy sauce in the other, served the lads and the girl, returned behind her bar, poured herself a *tsipouro*, and sat down with the guy. She sat at the chair that was between the guy and the couples.

'Here I am,' she said.

The guy made no response.

They drank their *tsipouro* slowly: Angie alert, scanning her customers, the guy's eyes fixed on the harbour.

'Let's have some more,' he said, and when Angie brought some more, the guy leaned in the direction of the married couples: 'How's the soup?' and quickly sat upright, gazing ahead.

The waitress's eyes met with the eyes of the couples, and the guy smirked. She moved her chair in order to obscure the guy's view of the couples, but the guy leaned to one side and, avoiding her block, said to them, 'You put plenty of pepper there, eh? I see, I see...'

The couples kept their eyes on their soup, the guy's pupils moving from one wife to the other: 'You like pepper, don't you?' and, once again, he looked towards the harbour, motionless, his lips puckered.

The husbands looked at Angie and Angie shrugged her shoulders, and the guy turned to the husbands and said that *they* should make sure that they eat the cucumber in the Greek salad, all of it. After that, he smoked a cigarette while the couples sipped their soup in perfect silence.

The couples paid and left, Angie cleared the leftovers, and sat back behind her bar.

The guy looked straight ahead, utterly motionless.

She lit a cigarette; he scanned his surroundings. She grabbed two small glasses; his lips puckered. She poured *tsipouro*; he smirked. She sat with him: they didn't speak and drank till their glasses were dry.

Three cars pulled up in front of the café. Eight men in their twenties and thirties got out and sat at one big table under the trees, across the terrace.

'Got to go,' she said.

'Fuck them. Stay with me.'

She laughed; he sipped his drink.

Order taken, she returned to him with more *tsipouro*, and he turned to the table of eight, screamed, 'YOU ARE VERY HUNGRY, AREN'T YOU?' and back to her: 'I'm a PAOK fan, from Salonica.'

And she, to him, aware of the customers' stares: 'What are you doing in Kavala?'

And he, to no-one: 'Constantinople must become Greek again. The whole of Byzantium must become Greek again. We must fuck the Turks. All Turks.'

'I don't mind Turks. I mind my locals. There's something wrong with me.'

'Got it,' he said, and, turning to the table of the eight men who still stared, he shouted: 'When your food is ready, make sure you eat all of it.'

Then they drank more without talking, them two and the table of eight.

'Angieeee!' a female voice called out from within the café, and Angie got up and sauntered towards the source of the voice and served the table of eight.

She sat back with the guy and he turned to the eight men: 'Oh, I see… You *are* hungry,' and straight back to her: 'I went to Constantinople when we played Galatasaray. I had a picture of Ataturk with me. When we entered the stadium…' he paused here, a big grin rose on his face, '…I made a hole in his mouth and stuck my cock in and shouted at their fans, "Come and suck it, Mongolian cunts!"'

'Did we win?' she asked.

'We?'

'I support PAOK, too,' Angie said.

'You don't support PAOK,' the guy said.

'Don't I?'

'No, you don't. You just say you do.' He smiled. Angie smiled, and brought more *tsipouro*, and the guy, towards the eight men: 'Take it easy with the food. Take your time. Don't *panic*,' and back to Angie: 'I'll tell you what my ideology is.'

'Tell me.'

'My ideology is that no-one should work. That's my ideology.'

'I don't mind working. But my locals make me feel uncomfortable. There's something wrong with me. Or with them.'

'Fuck them. Stay with me.'

From time to time the table of eight asked for more drinks, and then a few more customers arrived, and each time Angie had to leave the table the guy darted angry glances at the customers and said that they should respect a young girl who was trying to enjoy a glass of *tsipouro*, and time passed like that.

As usual, a large number of customers came when clubs and bars closed. Now the guy cast his eyes over the people as they arrived at the café and swore at them the moment they stepped onto the terrace. No-one sat under the gazebo, none said anything back, everyone avoided his glare. He was one and they were many and the many were scared of the one.

There were two or three tables waiting to order food. Having been verbally abused by the guy, they didn't dare to look towards the waitress.

'I'll be back soon,' Angie told him. She went into the kitchen and came out with a man of about seventy years old. They stood by the bar and Angie began talking and pointing at tables around the terrace and the old man kept nodding. Then she gave him a bunch of notes and some coins, and the old man took hold of the tray.

She sat with the guy.

'I've got a son,' the guy said. 'I don't know where he is. Maybe he's still somewhere in Salonica. The last time I saw him it was dawn. Like now.'

'But it's not dawn now.'

'It was dawn, like now. He was lying on a pavement, in a busy street. He was sleeping or he was dead, I didn't check. The needle was there. I put some money in his pocket and told him, "Good luck, friend."' He downed his *tsipouro* and finished it.

'Hang on,' said Angie, and she brought a carafe of the strong alcohol. While she poured from it, the guy turned towards the whole terrace and shouted: 'Oi! What're you eating there? Soup? What soup? Turd soup? Nice. Enjoy your turd soup, bastards,' and straight back to Angie: 'Don't worry, miss.'

'I'm not worried.'

Customers came and went, the old man struggling to keep up, but never asking Angie for help. Only, sometimes, he looked towards her, with a smile.

There was a bit of *tsipouro* left in the carafe when two policemen approached, one middle-aged, stout, with a thick moustache; the other in his early twenties. As soon as the guy spotted the policemen, he began panting. Thick veins bulged on his forearms and biceps as he grabbed the arms of his chair and squeezed them. His lips puckered. And when the policemen went to take a seat, the guy jolted off from his chair and screamed: 'GO FUCK YOURSELVES, YOU FUCKING PIGS,' then sat back and turned to Angie, breathing heavily: 'Don't be scared. I'm here with you. I'll clean up the mess. Don't be scared, miss,' and cocked his eyes forward, the panting dying down.

'Come again? What did you just say?' the middle-aged policeman said, standing a yard diagonally behind the guy.

The guy got up, turned around, and pushed his face into the policeman's: 'Watch your tongue, pig.'

'What's your problem?'

'I'll fuck you, slime. Pig.'

'Calm down or I'll take you to the station,' the policeman said, stepping back.

'You think I'm scared of you, cunt?'

'Calm down or you'll be in trouble, mate.'

'I'm not your mate. I'm not friends with pigs. Pig...'

The policeman walked away and sat with his colleague five tables away—diagonally behind the guy's back.

Smiling, the old man served the policemen chicken soup, and then, without being asked to, he refilled Angie's carafe with *tsipouro*. They drank half of the carafe while the guy kept threatening the policemen that he would take from behind their mama-pig and baba-pig and suggesting that they should top up their plates from the toilet bowl. After each insult, the guy turned to Angie saying that she shouldn't worry, that he was there for her, no matter what.

The policemen left and many other customers left, and he and Angie looked straight ahead. Far away in the darkness of the sea, lights from the returning caïques shone.

'Don't you like watching the fishing trawlers returning to the harbour?' she asked.

The guy made no response.

'Or do you prefer it when they sail away?'

No answer.

Time passed with the guy insulting the few remaining customers, while Angie ignored the guy and the customers and looked ahead, doing what she liked the most during her night shifts, watching the lit caïques returning, imagining.

By the time the first caïque moored, there were no more customers left in Café Papaya, and now it was dawn in the small town of Kavala.

'And now it is dawn in your big city, too.'

The guy stared at her as her lips gavé an ironic curl.

More caïques moored. Two Egyptian fishermen crossed the cobbled street and sat under the gazebo. One was blond, handsome and young, same age as Angie maybe, with big green eyes, the only one of the Egyptians in the harbour who had blond hair. The other was older, similar age as the guy.

Seven Greek fishermen, captains and second captains and *lambadoros*, sat by a table in the far corner of the terrace.

The guy fixed his eyes on the Egyptians, who ordered hot coffee.

When their coffee was served, the Egyptians began talking in their language.

'This is Greece. What're you doing here in Greece?' said the guy.

The older Egyptian looked down, but the young, blond one, cast a stealthy glance at the man who had addressed them.

Angie caught the eye of the young Egyptian and motioned for him to remain seated.

Keeping his eyes fixed on the blond Egyptian, the guy turned towards Angie and sneered: 'All foreigners must go away.'

Then Angie spoke. 'I know these guys. Leave them alone. They aren't policemen. They aren't the locals. They are the weak ones, like you.'

'Oh, come on now, miss. I'm just teasing them.'

'They don't like to be teased. They are the weak ones, like you and me.'

'I won't do it again.'

The old Egyptian raised his coffee mug, had a sip, put it down. The guy raised his glass, his lips puckered, had a sip, put it down. Angie raised hers, had a sip, waited; the blond Egyptian raised his, had a sip—they put them down together.

23

And then the guy gave the finger to the young Egyptian. He did it in the most vulgar way, common amongst Greeks and Arabs, and, winking to the blond Egyptian, he said: 'Fancy a quickie?'

The Egyptian rolled his big, green fierce eyes at him and twisted his hand with a motion that said, 'What's your problem?'

And Angie, to the guy: 'What are you doing now? I told you they're good lads, didn't I?'

'OK, OK.'

'Don't mess with them.'

'Oh, I'm sorry. I don't know why I did such a thing. Pardon me, miss. I won't do it again,' and, crushing the cigarette butt, he gave the finger to the blond Egyptian again, and the Egyptian dashed at him and grabbed him by the throat with such force that the guy's chair titled backwards: 'What you want?'

The guy didn't move, his small grey eyes stared at the big green ones without any sign of emotion, as if he was looking at the harbour and out to sea.

Angie got up and ordered them to separate and the Egyptian let go of his grip.

From the far end table, three Greek fishermen strode over and took hold of the guy and pulled him to his feet and pushed him with such force that he fell four or five yards away, on top of a table, crushing it. Before the guy could raise himself, the fishermen grabbed him again and pushed him further away, and then again, until he lay next to the road, on the pavement. They prepared their fists, but the blond Egyptian held back the Greek fishermen: 'No, Angie said no, if she said no, she must know something.' Everyone returned to their tables and Angie behind her bar.

And the guy stood up, his shirt torn beneath the breast pocket. He walked to the table of Greek fishermen and stood there, staring at them.

'Go away,' they said. 'Go away.'

But the guy didn't move.

A fat captain raised his voice: 'We've been watching you for some time now annoying the Egyptian lads. Now we tell you to go away. Piss off to wherever the fuck you come from. Why don't you go away?'

The guy stood there, staring at him.

'We're telling you to get the hell out of here. Why the fuck don't you go, eh? Why don't you just walk away, nobhead? Piece of shit? Cunt? Tell me why?'

And the guy stood there. Staring at him.

The fat captain stood up and, as he did so, his chair fell backwards. 'Oi! Get the hell out of here, don't you get it?'

And the guy stood there, silent, motionless, utterly motionless, in front of all the Greek fishermen, looking straight into the eyes of the fat one.

The fat man pushed the guy.

The guy tottered back two steps.

All seven Greek fishermen stood up.

The guy stood still against the violence of their eyes.

And they all laid their hands on him; and the guy fell. He fell without noise, silently. 'Go, go away.' He stood up, didn't move. And the fishermen tossed him aside and he fell onto tables and chairs. 'Go away.' They yanked him to his feet, and he stood on his feet, his face bloody. 'Just go. Don't you get it?' They pushed him; he bounced off a tree trunk, fell down. Stood up. 'Just go away.' He didn't. Fists and elbows and boots lashed out. He ended up in the middle of the street, doubling up, panting, his small grey eyes never closing.

Angie made a phone call. The Greek fishermen returned to their table.

A taxi came; the guy stood up and got in.

The taxi left.

Now it was quiet in Café Papaya. The Greek fishermen resumed their conversation and Angie had a friendly chat with the blond Egyptian.

With a nod, the old man took her to one side, handed the tray back to her, and his old eyes were sparkling: 'If he wasn't drunk, he could have done it.'

She cleaned the mess, returned behind her bar.

A taxi stopped in front of the café and the guy stepped out, went straight to the open bar, said to her: 'Get me a glass of water.'

'If you promise you won't do anything stupid with the glass.'

The guy was glaring at the Greek fishermen: 'I'm checking them over. Got to remember their faces. I'll kill them. Get me a glass of water, miss. I promise.'

She poured water into a glass and handed it over to him.

He drank half of it, tossed the rest to the floor, and stared at her, through dirt and blood: 'Is it still dawn in Salonica, miss?'

'It will always be dawn in Salonica.'

He bowed at her. Then got into the taxi, and never returned to Café Papaya.

Their Soupsoul Laughter Echoes Dreadfully in Empty Bowls

On a cold winter night Pavlo and the boss of Café Papaya entered a bar and checked the time: they had time. They drank a bottle of red and they still had time, so they drank three more and checked the time: they were one hour late.

'Boy! Bring us a bottle of red, will you?' said the boss. 'And be quick, boy. We're *late!*' He turned to Pavlo: 'What are we late for?'

'My night shift.'

'What night shift?'

'At your café, boss.'

'What time do you start?'

'An hour ago.'

'Don't worry. You're my best waiter.'

'I'm the best waiter in town.'

'You reckon?'

'Why do you think they call me Super-Tray?' Pavlo lit up two cigarettes and passed one to his boss. 'Boss, your eye is closed.'

'Which one?'

'The right one.'

'It's that fucking tomato.'

'What tomato?'

'I ate a tomato which couldn't have been organic.'

'Boss?'

'*Boss, boss, boss…* What is it, what?'

'I've got to go. Angie will be mad.'

'Who's Angie?'

'Your evening shift waitress.'

'Ah, her… I think she's stealing from me. Let's go. I'll give you a lift.'

They finished the bottle quickly, left the bar, and got into the car.

About ten minutes later the boss managed to put the key into the ignition. He turned the engine on, stepped on the accelerator, and crashed into a lamppost. His closed eye opened up wide. They got out and had a smoke, the car smoked too. Nothing serious though. They got back in and the boss fell asleep. Pavlo pulled him into the passenger seat and he climbed over him. He drove on the night streets of Kavala. Sometimes he drove on the wrong side of the road, but that wasn't a problem as the cars that came from the opposite direction drove on the wrong side too, and the boss woke up in time to give them the finger.

They arrived at Café Papaya, two hours late. It was empty. Angie handed in the takings to the boss and made to leave. The boss wanted to talk to her about certain issues, 'Come, take a seat, Angie, let's have a chat,' but, no, Angie had to go. The boss insisted: 'But, I'm the boss!' Angie said that she would be late home and her father and mother would get *very* angry. She had to go. Still, the boss wanted to talk to her. No, she had to go. She left.

'You never stay at the café, boss.'

'That's because I don't like my café. There's something wrong with it.'

'Stay tonight and I'll show you what a great waiter I am.'

'I'll stay then. Let's have some wine.'

Pavlo went for a piss, filled a litre copper jug with red

wine from the barrel, and they sat by the table next to the bar.

They drank and smoked and it was good.

Then they smoked and drank and it was even better.

Once the wine was gone, the boss's eye closed again.

'I'm a bit hungry, boss.'

'You can have whatever you like tonight.'

'I always do. And you?'

'I don't eat at night.'

Pavlo went to the kitchen, said hi to the lady there, turned on the cold water tap and put his head under it. He dried his hair with a tablecloth and blew his nose in it. A big bowl caught his attention. He opened a fridge, filled the bowl with *vrasto* veal soup, put it in the microwave, pressed some buttons, and watched the microwave's clock ticking down for four and a half minutes. He took a knife and demanded the lady's handbag. He got her brush out, brushed back his hair, and put her handbag in the microwave for three minutes. He had an idea. He opened another fridge, took out three portions of feta cheese, crumbled them over the soup, and put all his fingers inside his mouth, licking off the feta cheese. He sat with his boss and began spooning the soup.

Still no customers.

'This soup looks filthy,' said the boss. 'Get me a spoon.'

Pavlo got him a spoon, pushed the dish into the middle of the table and they ate from the same bowl. Sometimes their spoons clinked.

The boss asked for wine and Pavlo grabbed the opportunity to go for a piss and make himself a coffee.

They smoked and drank, and drank and smoked, and it was good and even better.

'Do you know what's wrong with this café during the nights?' asked the boss.

'No.'

'Don't just say no. Think about it.'

Pavlo thought about it.

The boss watched with his one eye Pavlo who thought about it.

Having thought about it, Pavlo said that he didn't know the answer.

The boss gave the answer: 'It's the lights. They're too bright.'

'Well spotted.'

The boss lowered the lights and they both agreed that it was much better like that.

Pavlo was sobering up, and his bright, shifty eyes began observing keenly all that went on in the café. Nothing was going on. Still, he was on his guard now, knowing that soon *they* would come.

The boss asked for a schnitzel with mushroom sauce, and Pavlo wondered how come the boss didn't need to piss when he himself had pissed three or four times already.

When the schnitzel was ready, Pavlo brought it over and the boss went for it.

'You like it, boss?'

'I love it, Super-Tray.'

'Can I try a bit?'

'Be my guest.'

The boss pushed the schnitzel into the middle, and they ate from the same plate. Sometimes their knives scraped against each other.

Still no customers.

The boss got up. Pavlo thought that he was going for a piss, but the boss took him by surprise and began dancing.

*

2.30am. Customers arrived. Two blokes. Pavlo eyed them up and down, turned to his boss: 'They are suspects.'

'Pardon?'

'All customers are suspects. They try to bring me down, to ridicule me. They like to feel they are superior.'

'Fuck them.'

But these two blokes were all right, Pavlo remembered serving them before and he knew that they were all right. They were exceptions.

He went to take their order, stood over their table, smiled.

They gave their order. 'One lamb offal *magiritsa* soup, one pork belly *patsa* soup, finely chopped, French fries, feta cheese with olive...'

'Excuse me,' said the boss. 'Don't you think it's too bright in here? Should I lower the lights?'

'Why don't you?' said Pavlo.

The boss lowered the lights and the customers continued:

'... with olive and oregano, and two cokes. And mayo for the fries.'

Pavlo went to his boss: 'Now shut up and watch me in action.'

The boss looked at Pavlo with his one eye as he disappeared in the kitchen.

Soon the kitchen's swing doors were kicked open and Super-Tray came forth carrying in his hands steaming dishes and bottles and glasses and bits and bobs.

The boss stood up: 'Magnificent.'

Pavlo stood in front of the customers and smiled.

'How charming,' said the boss.

Pavlo left the bread-basket at the table's edge, slid from his finger the hook of the vinegar and olive oil holder and left it by the bread-basket, and then he did the same with the salt and pepper holder, only he left that on the basket's other side, just to add a bit of beauty to the table. Here came the French fries, there the feta cheese.

The boss sat down. 'But how many hands do you have, eight?'

Pavlo turned to him: 'Pay attention now.' On the right side of the one customer he placed a bottle of coke and a glass, but he placed the other coke and glass on the customer's *left* side, and turned to the boss: 'Did you notice that our friend here is left-handed?'

The boss was about to start clapping, when Pavlo with a svelte move stood behind the customers, served the soups, and, finally, he left a jar of *boukovo* in case they liked it hot. And all with such manners, such politeness, and without a single drop from the soup having been spilt. Like an eel he slipped in front of them again and smiled.

'Ah, Pavlo, you smug bastard!' said the boss.

The customers thanked him.

'Oh!' He rushed to bring over a small bowl with mayo: '*Kali oreksi.*'

Having observed in the meantime that the boss's wine was finished, he filled it up and sat back down.

'You are a magnificent waiter, Pavlo. And the only Super-Tray without a tray.'

Pavlo didn't reply. He never talked while enjoying a triumph.

More customers arrived. Two guys, one girl.

This time Pavlo didn't eye them up and down, as he was still overwhelmed with his previous success. He stood before them, smiled, and, smiling, he said, 'So how are you tonight?'

'Trying not to get upset,' said one of the guys. He had curly hair, slathered in gel.

Pavlo laughed at this remark. He thought it was a joke. They didn't laugh. It wasn't a joke. They hadn't even smiled.

'How long for a carbonara?' asked the gel guy.

'No more than six or seven minutes, sir.'

'LAST TIME I WAITED FOR TWENTY MINUTES!' shouted the gel guy, banging his fist on the table. Now, if Pavlo wasn't working, if he wasn't a waiter, and a magnificent one as the boss had previously remarked, then he would certainly tell the gel guy exactly where to put that fist. But he was a waiter, so instead, he explained that last time it might have took him twenty minutes because it must have been very busy, to which the gel guy answered that he was on his own and the café was empty and it still took him twenty minutes to be served a single carbonara.

Bullshit, Pavlo thought. These customers were part of *them*, the vast majority, the arrogant, rotten townsfolk. Pavlo had a nose for sensing customers that were intimidating. Very well, he would be blunt with this table: absolutely *no* magic for them, ha!

'I reassure you, sir, that it won't take more than six or seven minutes.'

'We'll see about that...'

OK, we'll see about that. Now tell us what you want, gel guy.

'Two spaghetti carbonara, one tortellini carbonara, one baked *manouri* cheese stuffed with red pepper and bacon.'

'...stuffed with red pepper and bacon,' said Pavlo, who had the habit of repeating the customer's last words while scribbling down on his pad.

Did they want any drinks?

No, they didn't want any drinks. If they wanted any drinks they would have told him so, wouldn't they?

Right...

Pavlo went to the kitchen, uttered some unpleasant words regarding the gel guy, gave the order to the lady, and remained there to release his tension by taking six deep breaths using primarily the stomach muscles and secondly the chest muscles, which is the right way one should take deep breaths to release tension according to the *It's All Their Fault: How to Deal with Twats* book that he kept behind his bar. Then he went for a piss. While urinating, his instinct told him that the mayo guys had probably finished their meal. Quickly he shook his willie, went out (he did wash his hands; he always did), strode over to them, found their plates empty: 'Did you like it?'

They said they did, but they looked sad, and left a €1.40 tip.

Exceptional customers. Pavlo cleared their table wondering why they looked sad, when the lady shouted that the carbonara was ready and Pavlo served the gel guy's table, in six or seven minutes, exactly as he had predicted.

*

The gel guy and his friends had gone and the café was empty when Satan popped in, holding his massive plastic bag, as he always did, filled with porn magazines at the bottom and newspapers on the top. His flies were undone; they were always undone, for ideological reasons.

Under other circumstances, Pavlo would give Satan his free beer and double spaghetti to take away and another free beer to drink in, and would hand him a pen and ask him to sit down and not talk but to write instead, and Satan would keep raising his beer glass to no-one and would write around the edges of his newspapers, in beautiful English script, the names of drowned English sailors. But that was not the case now because now the boss was around and Pavlo had to turn to his boss: 'What shall I do with him, boss?'

Under other circumstances, the boss would give Satan €5 or €10, depending on how insistent Satan was, and would kick him out of the café. The boss's legs were now softened by the wine, though, and there was not a soul in the café.

'So, boss, what shall I do with him?'

'It's too bright in here. Lower the lights a bit more.'

As Pavlo lowered the lights, Satan smirked: 'Hello, every-one. This is Pavlo, a brave man, one of us. Pavlo, get me a beer and I won't utter a word. I'll be righteous, a gentleman, and a decent sort of chap.'

The boss called Satan over and gave him cigarettes. 'Here. But you won't utter a single word, eh? You'll be a decent sort of chap.'

'I'll be the epitome of decency. I'll be righteous, a gentle-man, and the finest fellow.' He went to the toilet for a piss and came out having pissed on his shoe. 'I was at the pussy-bars. I've spent all my money at the pussy-bars, Pavlo, my friend. On the whores. Pussy, pussy, pussy-bars. €100, €150, I've spent it all at the pussy-bars. On their pussies. For their pussies. Good pussies, juicy pussies… Pavlo, why don't you say anything, Pavlo?'

'I don't know what to say. Were they good pussies?'

'They were good and juicy and tender yummy mummy pussies. Get me a beer, Pavlo! At the pussy-bars! At the whores and the pussies I was. Pavlo, good lad, Pavlo, my friend, Pavlo, my everything, everything I've lost for their pussies, everything.'

'Is it Amstel or Heineken you drink, Satan?'

'Don't call me Satan!'

'Sorry. I thought that was your name.'

'They call me Satan to take the piss. They call me Satan because I look like Satan. They call me Satan, but I'm not Satan, *they* are Satans!'

These were not the only reasons they called him Satan. Pavlo had heard locals saying that when Satan was a young man, he used to hang around outside nurseries, always wearing a long, buttoned-up raincoat, and one day, when the opportunity had presented itself, he had slipped into a nursery where he found three little girls, all alone and all so pretty that he had raped all three of them. But that was only what locals said and Pavlo didn't like his townsfolk, he didn't trust them; but he needed to trust someone, so he trusted Satan.

'So is it Amstel or Heineken?'

Satan drinks Amstel. 'And get me a spaghetti with double mince and sauce. To take away. I'll drink my beer and I'll go.'

'Sit down,' said the boss. 'Tonight you're allowed to sit down and drink your beer. Sit down in that corner.'

'I will. I will sit down. But not in the corner, like the stale currant-breads. I want to sit down anywhere I fancy, like the rest of the people. No more social exclusion. Look, boss, I need strong financial support. I need strong, friendly financial support.'

'I haven't got any money.'

'Then give me a pair of sunglasses.'

Pavlo served him the beer, Satan took a swig and his eyes blazed: 'Pavlo! Get me *two* spaghetti!' but Pavlo was fed up of going to the kitchen and ignored him. This infuriated Satan who turned to the boss: 'Boss! Get me two spaghetti with double mince and double sauce and I won't utter a word. I'll be a gentleman. I also want the sunglasses, one bottle of perfume, and two yellow shirts, Dolce & Gabana.'

'I haven't got any sunglasses with me.'

'Then give me €10.'

'No way.'

'Then give me €20.'

The boss got up and grabbed Pavlo by the arm: 'Do you really give him two spaghetti and beers for free?'

'Yes,' said Pavlo. 'And he also steals any tips left on the tables for me and all the newspapers and magazines you buy for the customers.'

'So it's *him* who steals the magazines...'

Satan raised his glass: 'Rah rah hurrah to Café Papaya!'

'Hurrah!' shouted the boss.

'Hurrah to Amstel!'

'Hurrah!'

'Hurrah to the Conservative Party!'

The boss asked him not to hurrah the Conservative Party, when the lights of a car that was parking in front of the café's gazebo drew the attention of the boss's eye, and gave Satan his take away spaghetti, and kicked him out.

'But I didn't utter a word, boss...'

'Humans are coming. Now you have to go.'

'But, boss...'

'Don't try to sweet-talk me. Out.'

Satan protested a little, rather gently, with decency and style, like a fine fellow.

*

With Satan gone, customers arrived. In front of the window, two blokes waited to give their order. Behind them, a man had been served meatballs *youvarlakia* soup. In the corner at the back wall, another table waited to give their order: two men in their forties with a beautiful girl who had very short hair and an elegant long neck.

First Pavlo went to the two blokes in front of the window because they had arrived first. He asked them how they were. One was looking at the ashtray and didn't answer. The other one, who looked like an aubergine, said:

'All women are whores and sluts. Yesterday I wanted to sleep with a woman. To *sleep*. How can I put it? I didn't want to fuck, I wanted female company. So I call one and tell her so and she says why not and I go over to her place. We lie next to each other and I go to grab her arse and she pushes my hand away. We sleep. I call her again tonight and we lie next to each other and I go to grab her fanny and she likes it. But I take my hand away, I don't fuck her. First I'll fuck her consciousness. Hahahaha.'

'Very clever. And what can I get you, lads?'

'Do you get any whores here?'

'Lots.'

The Aubergine nodded towards the girl with the elegant long neck: 'She's a whore, too.'

'Is she?'

'Not that sort. She does it for free.'

'Fair enough.'

'She gives fine head.'

'It must be the long neck. So what can I get you, lads?'

'One fried *tigania* souvlaki in white wine and mustard sauce, one grilled lamb chops with fries, tomato-cucumber salad without the onions but with olives—*with* the olives—one *retsina*, one coke.'

'...one *retsina*, one coke.'

'No, make that two.'

'Make what two?'

'The cokes.'

'Ah.'

The Aubergine got up and nodded at the beauty and they went into a corner and talked.

How beautiful she was, how beautiful and how sweet... Pavlo stood behind the bar, waiting for them to finish arranging the blowjob business, so that he could take the order from the beauty's table. He waited and waited. What took them so long? He rolled up the sleeves of his shirt. He had big, veiny forearms, like Popeye's. They were the only parts of his body that he exercised regularly (by carrying plates); he wanted the beauty to see them.

'Don't think I'm drunk,' the boss said from his table. 'I am observing the way you interact with the customers. You're doing a splendid job. What was this man who looks like an aubergine talking to you about?'

'He said that all women are whores.'

'Poor lad. Imagine how much he must've been wounded by women. You know, those meatballs you served earlier. We must reduce their size, they look like the balls of King Kong.'

Pavlo saw the girl smiling at him and rushed to her table. They were ready to order:

'Two calf's head soups for us. And one boiled cow tongue,' said her friends. 'And be quick.'

'I'm always quick.'

The girl was looking at the waiter and her beautiful face was still smiling when she asked for a chicken soup and...

'... and may I ask what greens you have?'

Ah, how polite she was.

So tell us, Pavlo, tell *her*, what greens have you got?

'Radishes.'

'Lovely. And one portion of radishes then, please.'

He served them. More customers arrived and, with ease, he served them, too. Even more customers arrived and he served them as well, but moving slightly faster now. Lots of customers arrived and soon even more, and the café was now full and everyone viciously demanded this and that and a bit more of that with slightly less of this but loads more of the other instead, and everyone expected Pavlo to apologise, he could tell that they *wanted* him to apologise, they hoped that he would lower his bright eyes and hang down his head, and say, 'I'm sorry, I do all I can, but I'm on my own, you see,' when Pavlo walked behind his bar and slid his magic massive tray from under the coffee-machine and turned into Super-Tray and served them all—at ease and with gusto. They put more pressure on him: get me this, get me that. Aha... He grabbed his small round tray and with one tray in each hand he got them this and that, cleared away the glasses and empty plates, while bringing out from the kitchen various spices and sauces the customers demanded, asking them if everything was all right. No, it wasn't all right: more of this, more of that, quick! They wouldn't give up, they wanted more, eh? Well, they asked for it: Pavlo thrusted out all his eight hands and octopus-like he began serving two tables at a time, while replacing used ashtrays with clean ones and moving things around the tables to make more space for the customers, topping up their bread-baskets and glasses of water, and loving it all the way, because now they couldn't be arrogant towards him, no, they couldn't ridicule him, simply because he had to move too fast from table to table. So for some time he did a few more of his virtuoso waitering tricks, until he returned behind his bar, and smoked a cigarette, enjoying his triumph.

The beauty walked over and flashed a sexy smile: 'I like you. You are polite and so good with your hands. Would you like to be the fourth?'

'What fourth?'

'I love gangbangs.' She pointed at the four men waiting for her: her two friends, the Aubergine and his friend, the Courgette.

'You got four there already.'

'Sadly, one of them only likes to watch. Will you join us when you finish?'

Pavlo said nothing. And the girl kept her eyes on his for a little longer, she just looked at him with those calm, penetrating black eyes, waiting for the waiter to say something, until she turned her elegant neck and walked away.

*

Pavlo poured himself an orange Fanta and sat with his boss: Well, no, madam, no, Pavlo doesn't want to be the fourth, madam. Pavlo is the one, he is the best waiter in town, he's got the most fearsome flexors in his forearms, the passion of four men in one, got it?

All the customers had gone, but he couldn't be bothered to clear the tables: letting the girl slip away from his grasp had made him downcast. It's too late now, Pavlo, you'll never have her. And you know why? Yes, you do know why, because you were scared and because sometimes you're like *them*, arrogant and a coward, hiding behind a fake superiority. So what if she likes gangbangs? Your silence was insulting, man, you insulted that rare flower.

The boss grabbed Pavlo's orangeade and drank it. Pavlo looked outside: the car that brings the trans with the transistor to the café parked by the gazebo, but its engine and lights remained on. Strange.

After five minutes the trans with the transistor came out, walked into the empty Café Papaya, took a seat, and put her transistor on. She had heavy make up on, as she always did, and shadows were dancing in her eyes.

Her pimp stayed in the car, engine and lights on.

The boss asked, 'What is she doing with his transistor on?'

'She likes her own music.'

'Is she Albanian?'

'I don't know where she's from.'

Tonight she didn't want to eat. She usually didn't want to eat.

'Tell her to switch that thing off.'

'Let her listen to her music.'

Pavlo made her favourite coffee, a very weak cappuccino with loads of fresh whipped cream and sprinkles, dusted with cinnamon.

'Tell her to switch that thing off.'

'She won't, boss.'

'Is she Bulgarian?'

He served her cappuccino. Usually she didn't smile. To-night she smiled.

Her pimp got out of the car and sat with her: a sixty-year-old man, a short man who always wore a black leather jacket. When Pavlo went to take the pimp's order, the trans with the transistor said, 'Is there any aspirin in this place? My head aches.'

Pavlo searched, no aspirin. 'I'm sorry.' He stood with his order-pad and pen.

The trans with the transistor said, 'My head aches.'

'No, it doesn't,' said her pimp.

'It aches so badly. My head.'

The pimp pulled down the zip of his jacket and held its one side open. A gun was there. OK, Pavlo saw it. His jacket fell back into place and he grabbed the trans with the transistor by the hair and slammed her head into the table. The cappuccino cup danced on the saucer. He pulled her head back up.

He said, 'Do you know what the time is?'

'It is always midnight in Moskva,' she said.

And he slammed her head into the table. The cappuccino cup danced on the saucer and the transistor fell flat. As he forced her back up, a horrible tearing sound was heard and a tuft of hair stayed within his grip. He wiped the hairs onto her face and grabbed another tuft and slammed her against the table. He raised her head:

'I asked: Do you know what the time is, tranny-fanny?'

'It is always midnight in Moskva.'

And the cappuccino cup kept dancing, as the trans and the transistor fell.

*

The pimp dragged her into the car.

Pavlo went to call the police.

'The pimp *is* the police,' said the boss. 'He works with the police. Don't bother.'

He put her transistor in a cupboard, swept the floor clean of hairs with bloody roots, mopped up, went to the toilet and vomited.

The boss continued his wine marathon.

Café Papaya was empty once more. Nearly 5am now.

The lady in the kitchen was doing some washing up.

The boss said, 'She makes too much noise.'

'It's the plates,' Pavlo said.

'That's another thing that's wrong with my café. Go and tell her to wash up the plates quietly.'

'Are you joking?'

'No. Go on, tell her.'

'It's not the washing up. It's putting the washed-up plates on the drier that makes the noise.'

'Then tell her to put the plates on the drier quietly.'

'You really want me to tell her that?'

'Yes.'

Pavlo told her. He told her that it was the boss who had said so.

*

Next came the powdered-up lass in black who worked in the local Gothic pussy-bar and who only ate a little bit of her meal as she had severe IBS, the poor girl.

She ordered a schnitzel with sauce and went to the toilet. After she returned, she asked for a lighter and Pavlo gave her the boss's lighter.

The lady of the kitchen screamed that the schnitzel was ready. Coming out of the kitchen, Pavlo saw the boss approaching the girl. As he reached out his hand to serve the dish, the boss snatched the schnitzel and ran away.

Pavlo went after him: 'No, no. That's not for you. You want your lighter. This is a plate.'

'I want it.'

'That's not what you want. Let it go.'

'But I'm the boss!'

'I'm sorry about that, madam.'

'It's OK.'

'He's my boss, you see. He's a bit dizzy.'

'It's OK.'

'Are you sure it's OK, madam?'

'It's OK. But do me a favour, please. Don't call me madam. I'm a whore.'

'Oh, pardon me.'

*

Having eaten a bit of her schnitzel, the girl left and the boss dashed to her table, finished it, and dozed off.

The door opened, and Satan, walking on tiptoes, approached the waiter and whispered: 'Never become a sailor, never travel far, it'll kill you, and when you're re-born you'll already be dead once.' Pavlo found that poetic and gave him two Amstels. Satan asked for one more, got it, and tiptoed his way out.

The boss woke up: 'I'd like a bit of wine. Please bring me wine.'

Pavlo brought him the wine.

Two caïques returned to the harbour, and three Egyptian fishermen entered the café. They sat in a corner. They were Mohammed, Mohammed, and Mohammed. They ordered beers and drank and talked in their language.

'They've turned my café into an Egyptian colony,' said the boss.

Pavlo laughed. He thought the boss was joking.

The boss was joking, but only half-joking. 'This is another thing that is wrong with my café: all these filthy Egyptians from the caïques who come here and give me a bad reputation. My café is an Egyptian colony. I must do something about that.'

Pavlo didn't laugh now. He got the half-serious bit, and looked at his boss suspiciously.

*

BLONG!
BLANG BLANG...
BLONG...
GANG! BANG!

The radiators stopped working.

Four men in suits entered and sat apart from the Egyptians. Pavlo apologised about the heating.

One of them said, 'We've heard that you serve *patsa* soup here.'

'That's right,' Pavlo replied.

'Yes, you see, we *all* want *patsa*.'

Oh, no, they were *patsa* soup enthusiasts… Stay cool, Pavlo. They'll try to intimidate you with their knowledge of *patsa* soup, but you can handle them. Stay cool.

'I see,' said Pavlo, and opened his order-pad. He flicked the pages of his pad, found a blank one, raised his eyes, clicked his pen: 'What sort of *patsa*?'

The four suits exchanged glances. They didn't expect such a cool reaction.

Pavlo waited.

They exchanged more glances.

Pavlo drew a willie on his pad: 'I'd like to know, a) if you want leg or belly or mixed leg and belly *patsa* meat in your soup, and, b) how would you like it chopped: finely, regular, or chunky?'

The four suits crouched and had a mini meeting, murmuring.

They sat back.

The first suit spoke: 'Leg. Finely chopped.'

'…finely chopped,' Pavlo repeated, and wrote it down. It was just his habit, but the first suit maybe thought that Pavlo was sarcastic and changed its mind:

'No. I meant chunkily chopped.'

'…chunkily chopped,' repeated Pavlo.

'Yes, that's it. Yes, chunkily chopped.'

'OK. Got it.'

The second suit spoke: 'Leg and belly mixed. Regular chopped.'

'Make that two,' the third suit chipped in.

Now it was time for the fourth and final suit to decide. It exchanged glances with the three others.

There was silence.

Pavlo clicked his pen to break the silence.

There was tension.

He clicked his pen to add to the tension.

The first suit leaned towards the fourth suit, whispered something in its ear, smirked, and sat back.

A glimmer of light sparked in the final suit's eyes: 'Leg. Chunkily chopped.'

The second and third suits murmured something.

'So that's all?' Pavlo asked.

Yes. They all sat back and loosened their ties.

The lady of the kitchen was sitting in a chair, peeling a massive potato. Pavlo tore the order from his pad, gave it to her, and apologised about the drawing. As soon as she read it, the potato slipped from her hand and, *plop!*, it fell into the bucket with the water: 'We've only got one portion of leg left.'

'WHAT DID YOU SAY?'

'I'm sorry...'

She left her chair and Pavlo sat on it. He took six deep breaths, the way it was described before. 'Only one leg portion left...' A terrible thought crossed his mind: 'Hang on. I only served one *patsa* leg tonight. How many days old is the *patsa* meat?'

The lady of the kitchen lowered her eyes.

'Look me in the eyes and tell me, how old?'

'It's ten days old. The boss said we must sell it before he orders more. He asked me not to tell you anything about it.'

Pavlo grabbed a peeled potato and crushed it in his fist.

'Please, don't act like that. You scare me.'

'So that's what the boss said, eh?' He walked out looking for him: he wasn't at the table. He went in the toilet: he wasn't there either. He went over to the four suits, hung his head, and broke the bad news.

They frowned and murmured.

Pavlo strongly suggested that they don't order *patsa*, but they ignored him. They wanted *patsa*.

Pavlo gave the new order to the lady in the kitchen, opened a 7UP, and sat down. The boss crawled out from under the table, went behind the bar, switched a couple of lights off, said, 'Much better like that,' drank a McFarland beer that was off, sat down with Pavlo and fell asleep.

And the lady of the kitchen got her big, steal chopping-knife and her big, wooden chopping-board, and began chopping the *patsa* meat, and everyone hushed. Pavlo hushed, and stubbed his cigarette out. The three Mohammeds hushed, and put their beers down and listened. The four suits hushed, and closed their eyes in pleasure:

CHOP! CHOP! CHOP! CHOP! CHOP!

The lady in the kitchen chopped the *patsa* into chunks.

chop-chop-chop-chop-chop!
           chop-chop-chop!
                   chop-chop-
chop-chop-chop!
           She chopped it finely now.

Chop, chopchop, CHOP.
           Chop, chopchop, CHOP
came the sound for the regular *patsa*. Then, again, for
           the second regular:
                   Chop-

The boss woke up: 'You're making too much noise!'

> ...*chopchop, CHOP.*
> *Chop, chopchop, CHOP ...*

*

Oh, God, no, not them...
I'm sorry, Pavlo, but here they are.
Not them. I wish they never came here.
Come on, Pavlo, get up.
He got up.
There were eight of them.
He got ready to take their order.
They got ready to take the piss.
He got ready to avoid the piss.
'Hi...'
First they insisted that he had previously cheated them on the size of portions, that the meat portions got smaller and smaller every time they came to the café, which of course was a lie. They demanded bigger portions.
No need to argue with them, Pavlo.
'All right,' Pavlo said, 'bigger portions. Now what can I get you?'
Well done, Pavlo.
They started giving their order. The first, the second, the third, the fourth. The fifth asked for a beef burger.
'Is that with cheese?'
'Yes.'
Pavlo wrote it down.
'No, without cheese.'

Pavlo deleted the cheese.

'With cheese.'

OK, he added cheese.

'I've changed my mind. No cheese.'

Right.

'With cheese.'

For God's sake.

'Without cheese.'

'Can you please tell me, with cheese or without cheese?'

'With cheese, without cheese. With cheese, without cheese.'

They laughed. Pavlo laughed a bit, too. Just to get along with them.

'All right. So do you want it with cheese?'

'With cheese, without cheese.'

They laughed. Pavlo didn't laugh. He moved on to the next one: 'What would you like?'

The previous one answered: 'I want my burger with cheese *and* without cheese.'

'OK, I'll put half a slice of cheese.'

Pavlo went to the kitchen, and gave the order to the lady. She read it. 'We've run out of sliced cheese for burgers.'

'Eh?'

'I'm sorry.'

Ah, lady of the kitchen, if only you had been a bit more prepared. There was no point in arguing with the lady of the kitchen. Pavlo went out, stood before them. His knees trembled.

They stared at him.

He looked at the burger guy: 'I'm really sorry but we've run out of sliced burger cheese. Would you like grated cheese instead?'

His mates stared at their mate.

'I love sliced burger cheese with my burger.'

His mates stared at Pavlo.

'I'm sorry. We've run out.'

They stared at their mate.

'Is that true or are you doing it on purpose to annoy me?'

His mates laughed. They stared at Pavlo.

'Look, man. We've run out of sliced cheese. I'm sorry. What do you want me to do now?'

'Shut the fucking place down! What do you say to that? No sliced burger cheese, shut the fucking place down!'

Pavlo so often wished that he was witty and with a clever answer he could turn things around. But he wasn't witty. He knew it and the regulars knew it.

'Don't be like that,' one of them said to the burger guy.

Pavlo hoped that that would be the end of his humiliation.

'No. I will be like that,' the burger guy continued. 'I demand to know why there is no burger cheese.'

And this was how it went for a bit more, until the burger guy, having enjoyed his success against the waiter, ordered grated cheese with his burger.

Pavlo sorted out their drinks quickly and sat down with the boss.

'What were they telling you?'

'To shut the place down because we've run out of sliced cheese.'

'To shut *my* place down? Go and tell them to fuck off.'

'Oh yeah? Why don't *you* go and tell them to fuck off?'

'No, no, *you* go and tell them to fuck off.'

*

The table of eight had their way with Pavlo, ate and left. Only the Egyptian fishermen were still in the café, taking their time with their beers.

The waiter spotted a man standing in front of the gazebo. He was a very big man, dark-skinned. He was giving wary glances inside the café, at the three Mohammeds. Something must have bothered him because each time he looked at the Egyptians he had to spit. He spat like that: *Aaaaack...PTHU!!*

The man entered Café Papaya, but now avoided looking at the three Mohammeds. He looked at Pavlo and the boss instead. And he talked to them about Jews, the scum of the earth. He talked and talked. The boss paid attention to the man, and Pavlo looked at his friend with more suspicion, then left the table and went behind the bar. He was scared that the man might begin talking about his favourite subject, how to turn immigrants into soap, so he made eye contact with the Egyptians and gestured to show that the man was cuckoo. They laughed. Pavlo laughed.

The man suggested that the boss should pay to listen to him talking because he had spent many years studying the classics and no-one could out-argue him, but the boss said that he had given all his money to Satan.

The three Mohammeds had kept eye contact with Pavlo, who had prompted them to cover their ears with their hands. They had found that quite amusing, and one of them, who was bald and had massive ears, did funny things with his earlobes. But the big man had a very strong voice, Pavarotti-like. He was saying that the Prime Minister was a puppet of the Americans and that they had to put his head inside an arsehole, that the other party leader was Stalin's granddaughter and they had to put her head inside another arsehole.

It was disgusting.

The three Mohammeds got up.

The big man sat down.

'Bye, lads,' said Pavlo.

'Goodbye, our good friend.'

It was only some poor immigrants like them, and rare girls like the one with the long neck who spoke her truth, and prostitutes or beggars like Satan, who were usually polite to the waiter. Maybe because they could see in his eyes that there was a fight going on, from the outside they could see what the waiter himself couldn't, that he was fighting his own townsfolk and was heavily beaten, and there was no chance for him. It was this lot who could understand him, and this understanding helped with the healing.

'What sort of breed are these mongrels?' said the big man.

'They've turned my café into an Egyptian colony,' the boss said.

'THIS IS GREECE!' the big man said. 'Make me a Nescafé: medium sugar, with milk. THIS IS GREECE!'

'Yes, make him a Nescafé,' said the boss.

Pavlo made him the coffee in a takeaway cup, and handed it to him: 'Do you know what the time is?'

'No, what is the time?'

'It is time for me to clear the tables and time for you to clear off.'

The big man shrugged like a little kid, and without a second word, he left.

Good, piss off. You don't want to see Pavlo letting out his anger, man, he can crush potatoes in his fist.

*

Lonely, the café stood in the harbour's corner, with most of its lights turned off now, almost dark, its heating broken down, cold, its suspicious waiter behind the bar, tired, its one-eyed boss downing wine, hammered, and its unprepared lady of the kitchen sitting lonely in the lonely café's kitchen; Café Papaya waited.

The door opened quietly and a Gypsy man stepped in. 'What's going on, chaps? Do you serve here? Are you open?'

'We're open, mate. Take a seat. What can I get you?'

'Get me a whisky.'

The boss went behind the bar and grabbed Pavlo angrily by the collar and shook him, demanding to know if this Gypsy was the one who stole the soap from the toilet.

Pavlo pulled the boss's hands off. No, it wasn't him. Pavlo had never seen this man before.

'Where are my car keys? I want to go,' said the boss.

'Take a taxi,' said Pavlo.

'Where are my keys, idiot? Give me my keys.'

'You're drunk. Take a taxi. And don't call me that.'

'I'll take whatever I like. I know you've got my keys. Give me my keys, idiot.'

Pavlo gave him the keys and the boss staggered out.

'Another one,' said the Gypsy, and Pavlo served him another one.

The boss walked back in: 'I can't find my car.'

Pavlo went out with him, and the boss got into his car, turned the engine on, stepped on the accelerator, and reversed into a lamppost. His closed eye opened up wide.

At the unlit part of the terrace, under a lemon tree, Pavlo saw Satan sitting in the cold, wrapped in shadows of madness, raising his beer bottle every time he called out a name of a dead English sailor.

The boss got out of the car: 'Thanks for letting me drive. You're an idiot. Go and make me a coffee.'

Pavlo looked at both eyes now, and they looked so much like the eyes of the gel guy, or the burger guy. In the boss's eyes he recognised the same sparkling light of fake superiority, he saw the eyes of the vast majority, of the mocking, rotten townsfolk. 'Go and make a coffee yourself.'

They said no more. The boss found a taxi and left.

Pavlo returned to the café. The Gypsy had gone. The new glass of whisky stood untouched on the table. Pavlo looked at the clock: 6.45am, an hour and fifteen minutes until the end of his shift.

The lady of the kitchen began her washing up again, and the waiter sat behind his bar, listening to the sound of clattering bowls that echoed around the café. He took a cigarette, lit up.

THE STORY WITH YULIYA HAS A BAD ENDING

What sort of café frappé is this, Pavlo, man? If I hold the glass near the lamp I can see through it—see? Say that again? Ah, it sort of settles after a couple of hours... Right. Make me another one. One and a half spoons of sugar, six drops of milk. Strong. Very strong. And bring me a jug of water with ice. I'm thirsty. Make the frappé very strong, eh? These bloody mosquitoes fuck my evening. Tell your boss he must do something about these bloody mosquitoes. And it's so hot, man. You know, Pavlo, why don't you quit polishing those glasses and bring your stool closer? I want to tell you the story with Yuliya. Do you remember her? Pffff... What a woman, eh? Russian. We used to come here sometimes for ouzo and meze. Really? You remember everything? What? OK, OK. Later. Don't forget the jug of water.

Pavlo doesn't want to listen. He says he's busy. What the hell, I'm going to tell him the story with Yuliya anyway.

Listen, man. She was such a beautiful woman, Russian, you know, tall, blonde. We were living together at my place. In my flat. I wanted to marry this woman. I knew. I understood. Me Egyptian, her Russian. Different cultures. You see, I let her sometimes go out for a coffee with her girl friends, but why did she have to work? I was working as a fisherman at the time. OK, yes, we went out together, sometimes she'd come here to the café with her girl friends, drink coffee, have ouzo, you know, nice, civilised stuff. But why did she have to work in a *bar*?

DON'T JUST STAND THERE! MAKE MY COFFEE! I'M THIRSTY!

I don't know, Pavlo, sometimes you're so slow. You aren't dumb or anything and that's why I talk to you, but sometimes you're so slow, mate. I'm sitting here at the bar because I don't like the other Egyptians. Only one or two of them are real men. The rest talk behind your back. They say I've done *things* back in Egypt and that's why I never go home. They can fuck off. Look at them, man, look at them, sitting around that table, miserable, hunched over their beer, one hand in their pockets so as not to lose their money, talking about the job on the caïque boats. They only care about money. Caïque, caïque, caïque, caïque. Fuck you and your caïques. I'm sick of the caïques.

Nice one, Pavlo. Thanks. That's fine, keep the change. Ah, I forgot there's no change. No problem, I won't keep topping it up with water and ice, it loses its colour, all right, I won't, whatever you say. You want a cigarette? Here, have one of mine. Bloody mosquitoes. Come on, man, stop that polishing, it makes me dizzy. That's the third time you've polished the glasses. You look gay with that cloth in your hand. I told you to bring your stool closer. I'm not going to fucking bite you. I want to tell you the story with Yuliya. What do you mean you've heard millions of stories, man? You're a bar tender, that's part of your job. I'm not like the others who come here and tell you their bullshit and break your balls just because they've nothing better to do: 'Oh I miss my country, oh I lost my job, oh my mummy, oh my grandma.' No, man. Morning, noon, night, I always think of the story with Yuliya. Listen, do you remember when Yuliya and I used to come here? What a woman. Yes, yes, of course. Later.

He says he's busy. Bullshit... Angie the waitress is doing everything. All he's doing is opening a bottle of beer and making a lousy coffee now and then, and putting them on her tray. And washing a glass or two every ten minutes. Right.

You see, Pavlo, Yuliya left me because she was scared. She left me and she fled the town. And she thought that I couldn't find her. Now, did she really think that I couldn't find her? I get hold of her number…

Bloody hell, I told him to make a strong frappé. What's wrong with him?

What's that coffee, boy? What's wrong with you? You call this thing strong? No, man. The fact that I'm tense doesn't prove that your coffees are strong. I'm always tense, for fuck's sake. No, I don't want a fucking chamomile tea. Put those aspirins up your arse. Never mind. Fuck it, I'll drink this one. Where was I?

So, yes, Yuliya leaves Kavala and thinks that I can't find her, but I get hold of her number. I call her. Once she listens to my voice, she shits in her pants. 'Look,' I tell her, 'are you trying to hide from *me*? What are you scared of, sweetie? I'm not going to hurt you. Come back and we'll talk it through. Nice, civilised stuff. Why did you leave like that?'

She didn't want to come back. I told her again, 'Don't be scared,' but she didn't want to come back.

Why, sweetie?

I find out from my guys, you know, the undercover officers, I know lots of undercovers, they're nice people, they're my friends, and by the way they know that you're a hashish smoker, so I find out from my guys that Yuliya ran away to Sparta and got a job there. In one of those, you know, bars.

Sparta, eh?

I go to see her friends. Two Ukrainian girls. They used to work together.

I say, 'You working today?'

They say they aren't.

'Then let's go and find my girl.'

'Where is she?'

'Sparta.'

'Haha! Are you crazy, Rasool? Go to Sparta? How can we get from Kavala to Sparta tonight?'

'Get in the car and don't worry.'

We get in the car. Sit comfortably. We begin. The roads aren't busy and I've got this special light on my plates so that the cameras can't read them. Because I go fast. Very fast. Bullet-fast. I pass by Salonika. Pass Thessaly. Pass Lamia. Going down down down. All the way down. Man! The girls saw Greece from end to end in six hours or so... Yes, of course, it's fucking possible, man, I've done it, we left Kavala in the evening, approached Athens at night.

When I'm near Athens my phone rings. It's one of my guys, an undercover. He hasn't seen me for some time and worries about me. He probably thinks, 'What's going on with Rasool?'

He says, 'Hey man. Where are you?'

I say, 'I'm here. Where are you?'

He says, 'Well, I'm here, too.'

I say, 'Good. I'll come by later on.'

I switch off my mobile and drive past Athens.

Now, what happens next is this: Mohammed with the One Arm passes by the café and my guy asks him about me. One Arm has heard that I've left for Sparta and tells him so.

'SHIT!' my guy says, 'CRAZY RASOOL IS OFF TO SPARTA!'

He goes straight to the police station. He says, 'Oi, lads!

Anyone got contacts with undercovers in Sparta? WE NEED TO STOP RASOOL BEFORE HE REACHES SPARTA.'

They find a contact. They call the contact. They say so and so. They say Rasool this and Rasool that. They pass on my details, the details of my car, and ask the Sparta contact to take care of me because I lose my temper easily, but I'm a nice lad really. They say to their contact that under no circumstances the police should let me inside the bar that Yuliya works in.

And I'm driving. Fast. It's night and I'm driving bullet-fast. With the two girls in the back seats. I enter Peloponnese. I see the sign for Sparta.

I'll find you, sweetie.

And just on the edge of Sparta, I see a police road block. As soon as I see the road block, Pavlo, I say to myself, 'This has something to do with my guys. They're trying to protect me.'

The police stop me.

I get out of the car.

I say, 'What's up, lads?'

They look at my plates. 'Where are you coming from?'

I tell them.

'Long time since we saw a car from up there in Sparta. Why're you going to Sparta?'

'Vacation. See Sparta. Just me and the girls. Is that bad?'

They let me go.

I reach Sparta.

I reach Sparta... Fuck. I need to find the bar now. Where could it be? I don't know Sparta. The girls don't know Sparta. We don't know the name of the bar. We don't know where to find it.

I know *how* to find it.

'Watch out for policemen,' I say to the girls.

I drive around the town centre.

'POLICE, POLICE!' scream the girls, 'POLICE, POLICE!'

Fucking hell. They almost made me deaf...

'Why are you screaming, sweeties?'

'Rasool! Be careful of the police, Rasool.'

I drive near the police. I park.

'What are you doing, crazy Rasool?'

'Don't worry, sweeties.'

I get out of the car.

The policemen come over to me.

'What's up, lads?' I say.

'Where are you going to?'

'I'd like to have a drink. In a bar. I'm on vacation, you see. Just me and the girls.'

'Do not enter the bar.'

'Which bar?'

'That bar.'

'Ah *that* bar? But why? Look, guys. We aren't going to do anything wrong. Just one drink. Nice, civilised stuff. Just me and the girls.'

'All right,' they say. 'But we'll be waiting outside. If anything happens, if *anything* happens, we'll take you straight to the police station.'

'Nothing will happen. Don't worry.'

They let me go.

We enter the bar.

Yuliya sees me and shits in her pants.

She's behind the bar. She says something to her boss.

The boss comes over to me.

I say, 'I'm not talking to you. I want the girl.'

'The girl can't come over. She's busy.'

I say, 'I've nothing to say to you. Send over the girl.'

'I told you she's busy.'

I say, 'LOOK. I'M NOT GOING TO SAY IT AGAIN. I WANT *HER* TO SERVE ME. *HER!*'

'I'll send you another girl.'

'I want *her.*'

'Can't send her.'

And he goes to grab me.

'DON'T YOU FUCKING TOUCH ME OR I'LL SMASH UP YOUR FUCKING BAR.'

He goes to jerk me out of my seat and I jump up and push him off and smash whatever's in front of me and throw tables and kick chairs and chuck ashtrays and shout: 'I'M GOING TO KILL YOU, YULIYA! DON'T YOU KNOW IT?'

Police come in.

They grab me.

They take me to the station.

They say Yuliya will sue me.

They say her boss will sue me.

They say they'll get me a lawyer.

But this doesn't matter, cause they say I'll go to prison anyway.

I make a phone call.

They change their mind.

They say they know I'm a nice lad really.

They say I must leave Sparta first thing tomorrow morning.

They say, '*You* must leave Sparta first thing tomorrow morning.'

That's what they say.

'I'll come back here after I've killed her.'

That's what I say.

But they let me go.

I find a hotel for the girls to sleep.

I don't sleep.

I wait for the morning.

Morning comes.

I wait for the night.

Night comes.

I put the girls in the car. Drive past the bar. Slowly. It's closed. I get out of the car. Approach the bar. It's dark.

I press my face up against the window. It's pitch black, there's no-one there.

The girls say they need to go back to work. They say they're tired.

I press my hands against the glass to stop the glare of the reflections.

Where are you, sweetie?

The girls want to go back home. They moan.

My nose bends against the glass.

Don't be scared, sweetie.

The girls moan. They need home.

I press harder against the glass, I feel it on my lips, I press harder, harder, my lips flatten against the glass—and I stay like that, staring into the darkness…

'Oh, Rasool, Rasool, don't act like that, Rasool!' scream the girls.

And I see a shadow moving… It moves quickly, from one corner to the other, as if someone is sliding along the floor.

I go to the door. It's locked. I smash the lock, get inside.

I can't find the light switch. I feel my way in the darkness, stamping my feet on the floor: 'Yu-uuuuliya… Are you trying to hide from me, Yuliyaaaaa?'

I hear a screech. I feel pain on my calf. It's a sharp pain. I get my lighter, strike it, look down. It's a cat. I'd stepped on her tail. Her teeth have sunk into my flesh. She won't let go. I kick her away.

I sit down, light a cigarette. I need to think. The cat comes to me, bites my other calf. She's a fucking crazy cat. I kick her away. She comes back. She's nuts. I grab her from the neck, strike my lighter. I bring the flame near her face, she stares at me, she shows me her teeth, hisses, she scratches my face with her claws. I walk around, with the cat in my hand. Her flesh feels soft and warm in my grip, I like it. I walk, feeling my way in the dark. I come across a freezer. I open the freezer door, shove the cat in, shut the door.

I sit down, smoke.

The girls call out to me, 'Please, Rasool, please get out of there. Please let's go back.'

'Don't worry, sweeties. I just need to think for a moment.'

I finish my smoke, get in the car, we leave Sparta.

When we're near Athens, I stop the car. I turn around, drive back.

'What are you doing, Rasool?'

'I forgot the cat in the freezer.'

'What cat?'

'I put a cat in the freezer. I must get her out of there.'

'Please don't talk like that, Rasool. Please, you scare us.'

'You don't need to be scared, sweeties… I put a little cat in the freezer because she annoyed me. I've got to get her out.'

'Oh, don't talk like that, Rasool…'

I think of the cat's flesh. I drive fast. How soft she was, man... How warm she was, that's what I think. How warm and how light and I drive very fast, bullet-fast, and I enter Peloponnese again and the girls scream and I pass Corinth and they cry and I pass Argos and Tripoli, and take the exit for Sparta.

I'm coming, little kitten. I'll save you, I'll give you to Yuliya.

I reach Sparta. I find the bar. Park. I enter the bar, open the freezer.

The cat is frozen.

'Girls, can you write Russian?'

'Yes, we can, Rasool.'

I ask them to write down: *I love you, Yuliya. Rasool.*

I stick the note with the Russian writing on the freezer and we leave Sparta.

And that's it, Pavlo, that's the story with Yuliya.

Well, say something, man...

What is it? I want the truth. I don't know, mate, nothing extraordinary happened in the end. What about the cat? She was fucking crazy, I didn't give a shit about her. No, I didn't eat the girls on the way back, I'm not like that.

You don't like the ending?

Fucking hell, you're right, Yuliya is in Sparta and I'm here. Pour me something strong now, a whisky. It's going to be a long night.

THREE MOHAMMEDS

Not a soul in the harbour, night shift with leftovers on the plates and greasy glasses around the terrace, but he couldn't be bothered, he just sat behind his open bar and the moon with its stars wasn't bad and the harbour with its caïques looked all right and the voices that were heard were foreign, from the back they were coming, from town, they were the Egyptian fishermen, the three Mohammeds, 'Marhaba, Marhaba,' and they sat at the bar and told him with their roaring voices that they had just left a pussybar, and something stirred in him, like pain.

'Yeah, Pavlo, women,' said one Mohammed, as one of the other Mohammeds legged it to the loo, and this Mohammed was known around the harbour as Up-Your-Arses, that's how they called him, not the one who went to the loo, the one who was doing the talking, the one who said, 'Oh so beautiful women, man,' this one was Up-Your-Arses, and he said, 'There was a blond there,' he said, 'new at the place and her nails were painted red, I was getting hard, what wouldn't I give to fuck her, but she said, "No, no, I've got my period," and I said, "How about a blowjob, baby?" "No way," "No?" "No, no," so I said, "Would you like another drink?" "A triple vodka and coke," she said, and I saw they poured her just coke and charged me for vodka, and I said: "Can you give me a blowjob now?" "I just said no, didn't I? What's wrong with you?" "Can I touch your titties?" "No!" and my cock was hard but trapped downwards in my jeans and my nob was rubbing against the seat, I was in agony, and I said, "Why not, baby? Why can't I touch your little titties?" "They hurt, when I got my period my titties hurt, touch my thighs," but I didn't know what thighs were and I asked what thighs were, I said, "*Thighs*? What are *thighs*? I'm a foreigner, what are *thighs*?" and she took my hand and put it there, high up her leg, and it was warm there: "*This* is a thigh," she said and took my other hand and did the same thing, "And this is another thigh, for God's sake you don't know what thighs are?" and I hadn't fucked for a month you know, I squeezed them, those thighs, and my cock kept pushing against my jeans and my nob was rubbing on the seat and I couldn't help it, all that agony, so I came: "Oh, I'm so sorry, so *that's* what thighs are, eh?" and she took my head in her hands and said, "You've gone all red and shy! Oh why don't you talk now? Oh you're such a sweet shy boy!" that's what the bitch said, she didn't know I had come.'

'Listen, Pavlo,' said the other Mohammed, who was fat and bald, with massive earlobes, 'the truth is that it's not good that they go to pussy-bars and spend money on whores.'

Up-Your-Arses almost screamed. '*They*?'

'Yes, you two, of course, you and the other Mohammed, that's all you do, you go to these bars for the women, the Koran says this is bad, and what you do is stupid.'

This was even closer to a scream. 'Don't *you* go to pussy-bars?'

'Very rarely.'

This one came from between his teeth. 'Now you're annoying me, fatty.' He turned to Pavlo, and this one came from the heart: 'I love fucking. *Wallah* I go there every night of the *baedoz*.'

The fat Mohammed said, 'I come with you because otherwise I have nowhere to go,' and, he, too, turned to Pavlo: 'What can I do, go somewhere on my own?'

Now it seemed that Pavlo had to do a bit of talking, to say something, but Pavlo preferred it when he didn't have to talk, it seemed that the Egyptians took it for granted that he had been to pussy-bars, that that's what men do, unless they are homosexuals or there were religious issues involved, that's what they probably thought and if that's what they thought then fair enough that's what they thought, but Pavlo had grown up learning that pussy-bars were filthy, only those who couldn't get laid otherwise went there, the pervs, the mentally deranged, the fucked up ones, and he had never been in one, and that's why he preferred to stay silent now, that's why and also because he couldn't stop himself from imagining that blond with the red nails: red nails turned him on, on and on, and so he imagined the blond's hand on his cock, he imagined her hand making a fist around his cock, squeezing it.

Pavlo?

Pavlo looked up and his eyes moved from one Egyptian to the other, and he saw the guilt of pleasure in them and it seemed like they saw the guilt of no pleasure in him.

Up-Your-Arses turned to the fat Mohammed: 'If you don't like the pussy-bars then go somewhere on your own. Don't join me and *then* say that I do stupid things. Stay in the boat and read the Koran and play with your cock.'

'But I didn't spend all my money there,' the fat one attacked. 'I send money back to my family.'

Up-Your-Arses had nothing to reply on that as he probably did spend all his money in pussy-bars, so he seemed relieved to see the third Mohammed coming out of the toilet, and he laughed: 'It's this arsehole who spends everything there.'

The third Mohammed had only one arm, the other one

had been sliced off one night at work, lost in the Aegean Sea, and he walked towards the bar with this air of satisfaction that some people have when they leave the toilet, and he took his time to take a seat, and didn't go straight into answering Up-Your-Arses, he wanted to light up first, and the others watched him as he put a cigarette to his lips, they watched him taking his lighter out of his shirt pocket, striking the flint barrel, it didn't work, striking again, the sweet little flame lit up and the cigarette burnt with tiny crackling noises, and he puffed on it, sucking in a long blast, '*Alhamdulillah*,' and he left the cigarette on the ashtray and into the night rose beautiful ribbons of fine silver smoke, and who knows maybe it was because he only had only arm that he didn't give a shit and took his time: 'So tonight, Up-Yours, you didn't spend all your money?'

'Only forty Euros.'

'Which was all you had.'

Up-Your-Arses laughed and told Pavlo that that was right.

'You see, Pavlo? I told you,' said the fat one.

The Mohammed who had one arm looked at the Mohammed who had two fat arms: 'And you, *habibi*? Didn't you buy drinks for the whores?'

The fat one spoke to Pavlo again: 'But what could I do? That's a rule when you go to those kinds of bars. If I don't buy them drinks, they kick me out.'

All three Mohammeds looked at Pavlo now, they expected him to say something at last, to give a verdict perhaps, to judge them, but Pavlo didn't care about their commitment to their religion, they could tell now that he didn't care about that stuff and he could tell they liked him for not caring, but what he couldn't tell was whether they could see through him, whether they saw that he was judging not them but himself, that he was feeling empty, sad, inferior to these immigrants who had been enjoying the life of pussy-bars, who now sat by the bar, half-drunk, fresh memories glistening in their eyes, and the truth was that he didn't have the balls to go to pussy-bars, he was scared to push open their opaque glass doors and, night after night, shut them against his town's decency, he was jealous of them, of the immigrants, of their boldness, their adventures, but he wouldn't admit it, and he looked at them and they looked at him, and the space in-between was trapped in guilt, his and theirs.

Seeing that Pavlo was a bit slow in joining the conversation, the three Mohammeds talked between themselves, accusing each other: 'You bought them all these drinks, *I* didn't!' 'You did! *Wallah* I saw you.' 'Yes, yes, and I was watching you both...' until they started talking in Arabic, probably about how many beers they'd had, they talked in their language for some time, then Up-Your-Arses turned to Pavlo and, nodding towards the fat one, he said: 'He's an arsehole, Pavlo, he keeps talking about the Koran, but he's like us, he does drink alcohol and he does buy drinks for the whores.'

And Pavlo kept silent, hearing the voices of the immigrants calling his name from the hell of Islam, *Pavlo, Pavlo*, he heard them, *Pavlo, Pavlo*, but he said nothing, he hid behind the veil of silence and saw them searching him with their eyes, and he felt that they couldn't see him, as if the real Pavlo couldn't have been him, but someone else, someone bigger.

At last, he spoke the words of a bar tender. 'What can I get you, lads?'

'Beer for me,' said Up-Your-Arses.

'Beer for me,' said One Arm.

The fat one hesitated. 'I should have tea, but how can I have tea while they drink beer? I'll drink beer, too.'

And so he served them the beers and opened one for himself, and they all sipped their drinks and talked about something else, something easier for everyone, and in the space in-between there was dishonesty and repression, and out there there were the pussy-bars.

Two Arms

1

I t was night and it was October and it was cold for October. It drizzled. The terrace of Café Papaya was empty, silent, wet.

Angie stocked the fridge with beer. She had sold five Amstels and two Heinekens that evening. A piece of white cardboard covered the Heineken case. She put the cardboard on the bar, sat on her stool, got a pen, and began to draw. She drew and drew, and when she looked up, she caught the figure of a man emerging from the Port Authorities. It was One Armed Mohammed. Or just One Arm for short. One Arm was called One Arm because he had one arm. The other had been sheared off one night at sea. He was pulling up the nets when part of the winch broke, fell into his left arm and sliced it off. Gone, sucked away by the waves. His one arm waved goodbye to his other arm.

One Arm stood, gazed out at the sea, took the view in, gazed up at the sky, took the view in, stuck the remainder of a spliff between his teeth and sucked that in and kept that in and emptied his chest of a sigh soaked in sea-views and star-views and hashish. He walked over to the other side of the open bar, pulled up a wet stool, sat, and soaked his bum.

'So what can I get you, One Arm?'

One Arm didn't want anything. He was sad. No, maybe he wanted something. He wasn't sure. Did he want something? Hang on. Let him think. Yes, he did want something. Beer.

'What beer?'

'Any beer.'

Angie cracked him open a beer, slid over a glass, continued drawing.

'You want a cigarette, Angie?'

Angie didn't. One Arm did. He didn't have any. He asked for one, got one, tapped it against the bar: 'How about an ashtray?' Angie passed him an ashtray. One Arm coughed, excused himself, 'Well, I think I need a lighter now.'

'Do you want a mouth to smoke it, too?'

'No, I'll smoke it with my nose.'

'It'll hurt. Why are you sad?'

'This is a long story.'

'How long?'

'Long long long.'

'I finish at midnight.' She looked at the clock. Drew. Said: 'You got fourteen minutes. Is it more than fourteen minutes long?'

One Arm lit his cigarette. Sucked in. Hard: 'It's five and a half years long.'

'What story is this?'

'The story of my missing arm. I want the story to finish, but it won't. I've had enough. What's that you're drawing?'

'The map of Greece.'

'Where are we?'

Angie pointed, made a blob, wrote the name of the town in capitals: KAVALA. That made no difference to One Arm. He couldn't read Greek.

'I want to learn to read Greek one day.'

'One day you'll learn. So will you tell me the story of your missing arm?'

No, now One Arm didn't want to tell his story, he wanted

to talk about something else. Lately, he said, there was no hashish around town. He couldn't find any anyway. A friend of his in Salonica had some, had loads really, but One Arm was scared to go to Salonica. Too risky. He had to take the coach to go there. Police stopped coaches. Police searched passengers. One Arm was scared of the police.

Angie kept on drawing and One Arm watched her draw, sipped from his glass, continued:

'But tonight I was sad. I was sad because of this long story that doesn't end. So I went for a walk by the harbour. It was raining, but I like the rain. I was walking over there, at the Port Authorities place. I went all the way down. At the break-water's end I smelled something nice. I saw two young lads in the rain, standing in the darkness, smoking hashish. I want-ed to smoke, too. I hadn't smoked for so long. I went over and said to them, "Excuse me, lads. Do you think it's OK if I take a puff from the cigarette?" They said, "Take it all, friend." There wasn't much. It was below the middle. Five-six puffs. It was good though. And so I smoked a bit, *alhamdulellah*.'

Angie looked up at One Arm and down at her map again. Next to the town of Kavala she drew a spliff. It looked more like a canon than a spliff and it pointed to the South. She asked: 'Where do you come from?'

'From Egypt.'

'I know that. I mean from what place in Egypt.'

'From a village.'

'What's its name?'

'You won't know its name.'

'Tell me its name.'

'Ezbit El Burg.'

She wanted to draw the North-East coast of Africa, but

she had already drawn Crete near the edge of the cardboard. There wasn't much space. She didn't care. She drew the coast anyway. Egypt and Greece came closer. She smiled at that. Then she realised she had missed out some sea. She liked that too. She felt happy for the missed-out sea. Asked: 'Is it a small village?'

'No. It's bigger than this town. Four times bigger. Five times bigger.'

'Then it's not a village.'

'We call it village.'

'Whereabouts is your village?'

One Arm looked at the map. Had a thought. Sipped some beer. Smoked. 'It's where the Nile becomes the sea.'

Angie drew the Nile Delta. Next to it, she made a blob and wrote down the name of the village in capitals. Said: 'Tell me about your village.'

'My village is six hours from Cairo. Cairo is big. Seventeen or twenty million people. There's a great zoo in Cairo. In Egypt we have beautiful stuff, ancient stuff, the Pyramids. They are huge. We have the Nile. Nile is great. Nile is everywhere.'

'Everywhere?'

'Yes, everywhere. If you don't see him, you talk about him.'

'Then he's still a God. Tell me about your village.'

'There's nothing in my village. Just fish.'

'Then tell me about fish.'

'Fish?' One Arm gazed out at the harbour. He gazed out at the harbour for a long time and stubbed his cigarette out: 'Fish?'

'Yes, fish.'

He filled his glass to the rim, emptied his chest with a

sigh and sent it out to the sea. Asked: 'You want a cigarette, Angie?' Angie didn't. One Arm did. He pulled one out from Angie's pack, lit up, drank more beer, and said:

'When I'm twelve years old, my baba says to me, "What job you want to do?" I say, "I like the sea. I want to go to the sea with the caïque and become a fisherman." He says, "*Mashallah*, this is a tough job. Later you'll regret it." I say, "No, I want to go to the sea." So, I go. I'm a tiny kid. This is the first time I go to work and I'm very scared. The captain says, "Come over. You sit here and watch. Don't move from here till I tell you." I say, "OK," and I sit in a corner on the deck. Then we sail away. As soon as we leave the harbour and enter the open sea I feel nice, very nice. The sea is silent. But then I begin to cry. I want to leave. To go back. *Wallah* I want to go back. But it's forbidden to go back. I've got to stay for a week at sea. A whole week. Day and night. I cry! Every day and night I cry: "I want to leave! I don't like the sea! I want to leave!" And then I see the fish. I see how they got the fish out of the sea with the nets. The little fish. I like this a lot. It's like a game. I know I will like this job because it's like a game. Then we go back to the harbour and I go to my baba and he says to me, "Tell me now. Will you go again to the sea?" I say, "I want to go to the sea again, baba."'

One Arm lifted his eyes to the sky, uttered a sigh, and sent it up to the clouds, and the stars beyond. He remained silent. He only smoked. Then he said: 'I like to remain silent and only smoke.'

'Yes, it's nice. And so you became a fisherman?'

'Not yet.'

'Not yet?'

'No. Not really. Then I go for another caïque voyage and

when we return to the harbour the captain pays me. He pays me very good money. I'm twelve years old and I have so much money. Too much! What can I do with it? I'm so happy that I don't know what to do. So I go to another town, a big city, Dumyat.'

'How did you say that?'

One Arm repeated the name of the big city.

Angie showed him her map: 'Whereabouts is this big city?'

One Arm took a long drag from his cigarette and let it rest on the ashtray: 'Not far from the sea.'

Angie made a blob not far from the African coast and wrote the name down. Said: 'So when did you become a fisherman?'

One Arm sighed. 'You sure you don't want a cigarette?'

She didn't. He did. He pulled a cigarette from Angie's pack, lit it, saw his other cigarette burning in the ashtray, uttered a sigh, and having sent his previous sighs to the sea and the night and the stars beyond, he let this one hang around his shoulders. He remained silent for a while, took one of his cigarettes, sucked that in, kept that in, pulled one leg over the other, and let out a silent fart.

'One Arm, can you please be a bit quicker with your story? We got six minutes left.'

'Of course. Where was I?' He sniffed the air. It didn't smell.

'You went to this big city.'

Happy that his fart didn't smell, One Arm narrated the next part of his story with confidence: 'Ah, yes. So I'm twelve years old and I come back with all this money the captain gave me and I'm very happy and I don't know what to do and I go to Dumyat. You know what is the first thing I do in the big city? I eat a chicken dish. Really. It was delicious. Then

I go to the cinema. I watch a film and then I go out and buy some clothes, shoes, all new, I buy a ring, and then I go home to sleep. My baba is waiting for me. He's sitting by the kitchen table, like that—angry: "Come here, you. Where you've been?" Oh, no... I'm scared of my baba. I know I'll get a beating. He says, "Come here. Where's the money you got from the captain?" "I haven't got any money, baba." "Haven't got money? You got all this money the captain gave you. Where's all this money?" "I bought trousers and shoes and ate and I haven't got any. I only got these coins, baba." "Only these coins? Where's the rest?" "Gone. Flew away!" I had smoked the rest, but I didn't tell my father. I had hidden the cigarette pack in my sock. And my baba grabs me. From here—the neck. He takes off his belt to give me a beating. I bend over the table and my shoe falls off and he sees the cigarettes: "*Aman!* You smoke again, *haiwan?* You spent all your money and you smoke too?" Beating, beating, beating... For one week I'm not allowed to leave the house. No food either. But when my baba goes to sleep, my mama brings me a dish, and says, "Eat, *habibi.* Eat, my boy, eat. I won't tell your baba." I eat and my baba doesn't know. Next morning I go to my baba and say, "My baba, I will not do that again. I will go to work and as soon as I get paid, I'll bring the money to you." He says, "If you do that again, I'll lock you in your room." I say OK and I leave. I go for another caïque voyage and, when we return to the harbour, the captain says, "Here's your money." I say, "No! Give it to my baba. I don't want it, I don't want it!"'

They laughed. One Arm's laughter was *murharharhar*-like and made Angie laugh even more.

'The captain gives the money to my baba. My baba gives a little bit to me, so that I won't buy cigarettes. But again, I get cigarettes from my friend. You know which friend? Maybe you remember him. He used to come here in Café Papaya. The one with the long hair.'

'Ah, yes, Long Hair. Where is he now?'

'Back in Egypt. We've been very good friends since we were kids. He loves me too much. We used to smoke hashish here, too. Now he's back in Egypt and he calls me every night and says, "I smoked a bit of hashish and I want to talk." We spend one hour on the phone. Every night.'

'*Every* night?'

'*Wallah*, every night. Only he talks though. He tells me stories and I never interrupt him, because he's so sensitive he'll think that I don't like his story. I lie on the bed and I put on the loudspeaker, and say, "Now talk." He talks and I fall asleep. He's so funny.'

'Yes, he is. So tell me, after the beating you got from your father you became a fisherman?'

'Not yet.'

'But when did you become a fisherman, for God's sake?'

'Hang on. How much time we got?'

'Three minutes.'

'Three minutes? I'm stressed.'

'Don't be.'

'OK. Right. So: when I grow up a bit, I don't want to always be working. I like skiving. The captain keeps looking for me. He comes to my home: "Eeeeh! Mohammed!" *BAM-BAM-BAM*, he bangs the door: "Get up to go to work!" I pretend I don't hear. I don't want to go to work. "Eeeh! Mohammed!" He shouts, he shouts, he bangs the door, he gets bored, he says, "I'd better go," he goes. When the captain leaves, I sneak out and go to see my friend. The one with the long hair. The captain comes there, too, and keeps banging, but my friend likes skiving, too. *Bam-bam-bam*, the captain bangs the door, he shouts, he shouts, he gets bored, he says, "I'd better go," he goes. He goes back to the caïque, but he doesn't have enough crew to go out fishing. Many fishermen are like me and my friend, we all like skiving. So the captain can't go to the sea and he goes to the café and drinks tea. Next day the captain comes again to my home and I pretend I don't hear and he goes to look for the other lads, and they pretend they don't hear, so the captain goes to the café and drinks more tea. That's how it went. Because we work for one month, two months, and then we don't want to work. We say, "Forget it. We'll go out, walk around, see friends, go and buy clothes. When money runs out, we'll go back to the sea."'

One Arm had a sip from his beer and stubbed out his cigarettes.

Angie was drawing the Aegean islands. She wasn't sure where most of the islands were or what their shape was, but she drew them anyway. Her map of Greece didn't look much like a map of Greece.

And that's how it went for some time. The night-shift waiter, Pavlo, was late to arrive, and so Angie drew and drew, and One Arm just gazed at the night. Then he said:

'I can stay for twenty-four hours in Café Papaya. From here, from this little corner, the whole world passes by. I like to sit and watch the world. Everyone passes by here. If people come that way, they pass in front of Café Papaya. If people come the other way, they pass in front of Café Papaya. If it's quiet, I look at the harbour and the sea and imagine people in faraway places. And so I like it. I like to go and smoke some hashish, sit under the trees of Café Papaya, drink a beer, smoke a few cigarettes, and watch the world passing by.'

'So when did you really become a fisherman?'

'When I was twelve years old.'

'Then why keep on saying, "Not yet"?'

'Did I?'

'Yes. Three times.'

'You know what?'

'What?'

'It's such a beautiful night.'

'Yes, it is.'

'I love nights like this one. I like watching the people, but I like silent nights, too. Like this one. Just sit here and see the rain and the street and the sea. Have you finished with your map?'

'Getting there. I have to draw the islands. We have so many islands.'

'The first time I came to Greece I worked on the Island of Naxos. Make a blob of Naxos when you draw it. I've lived there, but I don't know where it is.'

'I will. When did you come to Greece?'

'The first time…'

'Hang on. Do you mind if I do the cashing up while you talk?'

'Is it midnight already?'

'It's past midnight.'

'OK, you do your work.'

Angie left her stool and stood by the till and pressed some buttons. 'I'm listening.'

'The first time I came to Greece it was in '88. I was sixteen years old. I came to Naxos.'

'Ah, of course, Naxos.'

'Have you blobbed it down yet?'

Like most of the islands, Angie wasn't sure where Naxos was. She decided not to draw Naxos. She thought Naxos was better off out there with that bit of missed-out sea. She said she would draw it later. Then she said: 'Go on, One Arm.'

'All of us Egyptian fishermen come to Greece with a work permit. For eight months. After eight months I leave. I want to come back to Greece, so I start doing the paperwork. But I don't have time because after a few days I'm called up to join the army. So I go to the army for three years. The army hurt my heart too much.'

'Oh really?'

'Oh really. Because army is like prison. Once I finish the army, like a little bird I go out in the street. And I come here again, to Greece, and go straight onto the caïque. From fire to fire.'

'What fire?'

'Army is fire and caïque is fire. I say to myself, "What the hell is this? Better die." I want a bit of life: buy clothes, go to the disco, go with, you know, women. I want to taste some of the good life. So when Christmas comes and we break from the caïque for four days, I spend all my money. Ha! Every day for four days I learn about the good life. Morning comes, I go out to drink coffee. Afternoon comes, I go to the taverna. Evening comes, I go to another taverna. Night comes, I go out with women. Four days. After that, I go to work. Then the eight months of the work permit pass and I must go back to Egypt. But I don't go back. I stay here. I was illegal for four years. And it's true, every day police were after me.'

'*Every* day?'

'*Wallah.* They shout, "Come here! Come here!" *Murhar-harhar.* Police. And I hide in the caïque. I go down below deck and crouch in a corner under a bunk bed and the police search all over the caïque for me and they can't find me. They leave, I get out of my corner, they come back next day, I go back to my corner. Ha! Sure, I was like a rat.'

Here, Pavlo arrived and took over from Angie. That is, he made a café frappé, dried a chair on the terrace and sat down to smoke. It had stopped drizzling. Still, everything was silent and wet. As if the land wanted to become sea.

One Arm sighed. Heavily: 'Time to go home?'

'I'll stay for a bit,' said Angie. 'Are you going home?'

'No! I'll stay here till tomorrow if you want me to.'

'Can I have one of my cigarettes?'

'No need to ask.'

They lit up.

Angie took a long, slow drag.

One Arm's mobile rang. He looked at the screen and a smile filled his mouth: 'It's my friend. The one with the long hair.'

'Ah, Long Hair! Say hi from me.'

One Arm put on the loudspeaker and answered the phone and talked in Greek. Introductions were made, then One Arm said to Angie that Long Hair was shy to speak in Greek because his Greek is not good and he's so sensitive about it. Long Hair said something in Arabic and One Arm told Angie that Long Hair had smoked a bit of hashish and wanted to talk. Angie's and One Arm's eyes met, and they smiled at each other. Then Long Hair laughed. He laughed way too long. He went on laughing for so long that Angie and One Arm found it funny and began laughing themselves. When all the laughing stopped, One Arm leaned over the phone, and said to Long Hair in Greek: 'Angie just finished work and she's tired and she needs to go home soon. We're smoking a last cigarette.'

Arabic came from the other side.

One Arm turned to Angie: 'He asks what we're talking about.'

Angie smiled. 'Tell him that I really need to go home soon. Tell him my parents will be worried. Tell him that we've got time for one cigarette. Tell him that we talk about rats.'

'What rats?' One Arm asked.

'Rats. When the police were after you.'

'Ah! When the police were after me and I hid under the bunk bed,' said One Arm, and told Long Hair about it in Arabic.

The sound of the lighter was heard. The lighter strike that came through the loudspeaker sounded better than the real sound, cracklier.

Long Hair spoke in Arabic. One Arm translated:

'He says that he wants to tell you the story of when he was a rat. He says he just lit his cigarette and his time runs from now.'

And so, Long Hair began telling his one-cigarette-long story in Arabic, One Arm translating in his broken Greek, and Angie listening and drawing more islands.

'He says that he spent many years as an illegal immigrant in Greece. The first time he came here he was sixteen. He had to go back to Egypt after eight months. But he didn't go back. He says he didn't go back because he has a mind of his own. He says every man has his own mind. His mind told him to stay in Greece and wait to become thirty years old so that he wouldn't have to go into the army. Because if you are away until thirty, you don't have to do your military service. You can pay it off, instead. That was his plan. But how could he wait for so long? When you are sixteen, how can you wait until you become thirty? How, eh? (I'm translating everything, Angie.) After seven years police caught him.'

Suddenly Long Hair stopped talking.

Angie looked at One Arm. One Arm covered the phone with his hand and whispered: 'Don't worry. It's the hashish that plays in his mind. He'll recover soon.'

Soon Long Hair recovered and the narration and translation resumed:

'Yes. So after seven years they caught him and sent him back. He was twenty-one.'

'It doesn't add up,' said Angie.

Quickly One Arm covered the phone again. 'Don't interrupt,' he whispered, 'he'll think you are bored of his story. He's so *sensitive*.' He continued:

'He says he doesn't want to try to remember if he was twenty-one or older, because trying to remember something forgotten is funny and he'll start laughing again and will lose time.'

Angie looked at her map. Next to the name of Ezbit El Burg, the Egyptian village, she drew a spliff. It looked more like a canon than a spliff and it pointed to the North. She wanted to make the two spliff-canons shoot bursts of laughter over the Aegean Sea, but she didn't know how to draw that.

'He says that it doesn't matter how old he was really. He says that police caught him at some point and sent him back to Egypt. Now he couldn't get away. No way. That was it. He had to join the army. But he didn't. He bribed some officials and didn't join the army.'

Here, Long Hair broke into a monstrous laughter. The night-shift waiter turned and looked at them. One Arm turned the volume down and begged Long Hair to stop laughing, but instead he began laughing himself.

When Long Hair began talking, One Arm turned the volume back up.

'He says his cigarette has nearly finished, so better be quick. After the bribing, he wanted to come to Greece again. But he couldn't come to Greece because he had been deported from here and the police here knew his name. What could he do? He changed his name.'

The two friends found this very funny and laughed with all their hearts. Very quickly this time, though, they quietened down, and continued:

'He says he changed his name and came to Greece again. He says he had chosen a shorter name, easy to remember, but, still, he kept forgetting it. About a year and a half later, the same story. They arrest him, they take him to the police station and put him in a cell. He grabs the bars and wedges his face between them, and wails: "What can I do, what can I do now? Ah, Allah, Allah, what can I do now?" The policeman tells him, "Don't be sad." He says to the policeman, "What do you mean, 'don't be sad'?" He was very sad. The policeman says, "What's wrong?" He says to the policeman so and so and so. The police know that we come and go illegally. So the policeman says to him, "Look, mate. We'll deport you. But you just change your name and come back again." He says to the policeman, "I've already changed it! Change again?"'

All three of them burst out into a final, hearty laughter, at the end of which, they stubbed out their cigarettes and Long Hair hung-up.

'Now I'll go home to think of my long story,' said One Arm. 'But when the morning arrives, I'll come to Café Papaya to drink coffee and watch the people passing by.'

'I'll take my map with me,' said Angie, 'and finish it at home before I sleep.'

'You still didn't finish? What do you need to finish?'

'I need to draw the sea.'

'How will you draw the sea?'

'With fish.'

'What fish?'

'Like the fish you saw on your first caïque voyage. Little fish.'

2

It was in the middle of the night when Angie woke up wet. A big stain had formed on her bedsheets. She touched her clitoris, took a deep breath, closed her eyes.

Ah… The night was warm and the sandy beach had the colour of cinnamon and the in the sky there were stars. A beach of fine ground cinnamon, and bright stars in the sweet black night, and silent sea with no islands, just sea. Angie stood on the beach and took all of it in. Then she stripped naked and walked into the water.

She walked and walked in the sea, but the water still only reached her knees, and she tossed and turned around in the bed. She splashed some water onto her vagina. That felt good. She took a breath, dived in. Suddenly, it got deep, and finally she began swimming in the night-sea. She was a good swimmer. She swam and swam, and there it was, ahead, not far, the new beach of golden sand. Ah, but this must be the Island of Naxos, she thought, and she felt something tickling the soles of her feet.

She went underwater and saw four huge calamaries right in front of her face, staring at her with their red red eyes, motionless, except for their tentacles and arms that moved slowly in a hypnotic dance. One of them had a strange tattoo across its body. It seemed the meanest one, it must be the gang leader. Two calamaries clasped her around the ankles and pulled her deeper down. The third went straight for her vagina; the leader shoved its arms down her throat. Angie choked, jerked in the bed, breathed, broke free in the water. She began swimming towards the Island of Naxos. The coast wasn't far. But her swimming was that of the desperate dreamers: slow, so slow. That made her panic. The faster she tried to swim, the slower she went. She looked back: four motionless calamaries with hypnotising arms in a cephalopod dance. She looked ahead, froze: a fifth calamary, even bigger, was speeding towards her, squirting ink behind it. They had encircled her. She felt the tickling again, the sense of being pulled down, and gasped for breath. Giving up, she closed her eyes in the pleasure of sweet surrender.

She felt something grabbing her by the hair and the sensation of being pulled upwards. When she surfaced, she jumped awake, gasped for breath. She opened her eyes and in front of her, in her bed, there was a bodiless arm that bled. She knew it. It was One Arm's missing arm. It was Missing Arm.

A sigh; eyes shut: sea.

Missing Arm strangled the camalaries, their arms still dancing after their death, and he grabbed Angie by her beautiful long black hair and dragged her towards the Island of

Naxos. He dragged and dragged and dragged and Angie quite liked it. When they reached the beach, Angie crawled on all fours and collapsed on the cool gold sand, exhausted.

Ah, how beautiful the naked Angie was. She knew herself how beautiful she was, and her knowledge elevated her beauty. She rolled on the sand, grains of gold sticking on her wet body, dressing her up in a summer night-dress. She whispered:

'You saved my life, Missing Arm.'

Missing Arm caressed her hair.

'Can't you talk?'

Vibrations came from beneath the sand, strong vibrations that tickled her bottom with pleasure. It felt like an earthquake. It felt as if the whole earth moved to give her pleasure.

Missing Arm scraped at the sand and unearthed a vibrating mobile phone. He pressed the loudspeaker button: a voice began talking, and although the voice talked in perfect Greek, Angie recognised it. It was Long Hair's voice. It was the Voice with the long hair.

It said: 'How can Missing Arm talk if he has no mouth, Angie? He can't even smoke. I can't smoke. We're cursed. I'd like to tell you the story of how we became cursed and ended up on the uncharted Island of Naxos.'

Missing Arm wagged a finger towards it, and the Voice with the long hair said:

'I won't tell the story. Missing Arm wants to know why you tried to kill yourself.'

'I didn't try to kill myself.'

'You didn't try to kill yourself? Then what where you doing in the Missing Sea, the most dangerous of all dangerous Seas?'

'It is a long story.'

'How long?'

'Oh too long.'

'We haven't got much time. Missing Arm is bleeding to death and I haven't got much battery. And, anyway, no-one likes long stories nowadays. Make it short.'

'Can Missing Arm hear?'

'Yes. He has developed a sonar-like system.'

'Well, then, listen,' began Angie, but the Voice with the long hair interrupted her.

'Hang on. Can you smoke when you tell your story? We love the sound of you blowing the smoke away. It's our fetish.'

Missing Arm scraped out from under the sand a cigarette pack, pulled one out, put it in Angie's lips, scraped out a lighter, lit it.

Angie blew away the smoke, and began telling the story of how she ended up swimming in the most dangerous of all dangerous Seas, in the Missing Sea:

'The story begins from the moment I leave One Arm at Café Papaya: I go straight to a kebab shop and say to the kebab shop guy that I want two gyros in pita bread that my father and mother had asked me to get. But then the kebab shop owner pops up from under the counter, a woman, and says that she has run out of gyros. I see the gyros right in from of me, but she says she only has two portions of souvlaki in pita bread. I don't know why, but she says it in German. She says: "*Gyros kaput! Zwei souvlaki!*" I thought that my father and mother like souvlaki, so I say that this would be fine. I get the souvlakis, don't pay—why should I pay a German?—and I leave. If only I knew what was about to happen next...'

Here, Missing Arm passed her the cigarette. Angie took a drag.

'So? What happened next?' the Voice with the long hair said.

She continued:

'After I get the souvlakis, I begin walking back home. There are no people on the streets, but I feel I'm being followed. I take the long way home. It's so windy that I have to tighten my grip on the plastic bag with the food in, as it gets blown around in my hand. Sometimes a strong gust of wind makes the plastic bag sing. The streets are empty, but I'm followed.'

'It must have been that German woman you didn't pay,' the Voice with the long hair said.

'I think so, too. I am scared.'

'You should have taken a taxi.'

'I know. Anyway. When I enter my home, I see my father sitting by the dining table, looking like that—angry: "Come here, you. Where've you been?" I'm so scared of my father. He says, "Tell me. Where have you been?" I want to answer, but words won't come out. I see steam filtering through beads hanging in the kitchen doorway, and I smell boiled meat.'

'What meat?' asked the Voice with the long hair.

'I think it was lamb.'

'*Alhamdulillah* it wasn't pork.'

'I know I'm late and my parents are very hungry and my mother has decided to make stew in her huge tin-pot, big enough to boil seven babies. I can hear the slow bubbling and the wooden spoon banging against the walls of the pot. It makes a terrible sound.

'Then my mother calls me from the kitchen: "Did you bring us food?" "I brought you food, mummy," I say. "She brought us food, mummy," my father says, and shoves his hand into the bag. He gets one of the wraps out, removes the paper, squeezes the souvlaki and the grease runs down on his hand, and he screams:

"'What's THIS?'"

"'It's a souvlaki,' I say.

"'She brought us souvlaki in pita bread, mummy!" screams my father.

"'Souvlaki in pita bread?" my mother begins screaming too. "SOUVLAKI IN PITA BREAD? But we asked for mousaka! We asked for MOUSAKA not fucking souvlaki!"

"'No, you didn't ask for mousaka, mummy. This is not fair! You asked for gyros. But the kebab shop owner told me she had run out of gyros. She said, '*Gyros kaput!*' so I brought you souvlaki."

'Then my father opens up the pita, and screams: "AND SHE DIDN'T EVEN PUT TZATZIKI IN THE PITA! NO *TZATZIKI!*"

'My father looks so angry. He looks animal-angry. It is horrible. I begin shaking from fear, my hands are trembling. I turn around to go up to my bedroom, when my handbag slips from my fingers and falls to the floor and my cigarettes fall out. My father sees them, and screams: "What's THAT?"

'I tell him that this is my cigarette pack and bend to pick it up. While I do that, I turn around and see my father. I know he likes it when I bend like that, and I love the way my flesh presses against and fills the tight cloth of my skirt. Anyway, maybe that's a bit too much information. So, I bend and see my father biting into his souvlaki and staring at my arse. He munches, swallows, and says:

"'You're coming back late and you smoke too, bitch?'"

'I tell him that I wasn't late. He points at the clock and says:

'"Do you know what the time is?"

'I look at the clock, but the clock has no fingers. "I don't know," I say. "What is the time?"

'"It is time to fuck you," says my father, and with that he stands up and takes his cock out. Ten inches long and limp!'

Here, Angie sighed and asked Missing Arm to pass her the cigarette.

'Was it really ten inches long?' asked the Voice with the long hair.

'And *limp!*' Angie added.

'*Allahu Akbar...* And then? What happened then?'

Angie took a few more puffs and continued narrating the events that took place in the dining-room.

'Then my father takes his balls out. They were big like satsumas.'

'What's satsumas?' the Voice with the long hair asked.

'Well. They are sort of mandarins, really.'

'Why don't you call them mandarins then?'

'Satsumas sounds better.'

'Were his satsumas hairy?'

'Very.'

'*Yiak...* We Muslims shave our satsumas every Friday. Go on.'

Angie went on: 'When my father takes his satsumas out, my mother screams from the kitchen: "Made in Uganda! Made in Uganda!" I'm not sure what she meant by that. Anyway. Then my father grabs me and makes me bend over the dining table. He pulls my skirt up, takes his belt out and lashes me. He rips my pants with his fingers, spits in his palm, rubs the saliva on his now semi-hard prick—which must have been at least thirteen inches long now, thirteen inches *at least*—pushes all the way inside me, and says, "Do you like it, daughter? You do, don't you? Has anyone fucked you like I fuck you? Has anyone been as deep inside you as me? Oh, I'm going to cum, oh, oh. Will you ever again forget to put tzatziki in my souvlaki, you little whore?" With each thrust, his satsumas bang against the table's edge. This always turns him on. He likes a bit of pain, but won't admit it, he thinks it's gay. I say, "Yeah, yeah, father. No-one has fucked me as hard and deep as you. Oh, you are the best. Oh, forgive me about the tzatziki," you know, this sort of stuff, just to keep him going. So my father fucks me and I'm ready to have an orgasm, when I remember something. Can you guess what the thing that I remember is? I remember that I had forgotten my map at Café Papaya. This puts me off completely. That's it. I know I can't have an orgasm.'

'What map?'

'The map I was drawing at the café at the end of my shift.'

'I'm sure you'll find it on your next shift. So, tell us, what happened next?'

'So my father is raping me and he still goes on about the bloody mousaka for God's sake! Then I hear glass jars rattling in the kitchen. Soon I smell oregano. I know my mother is finishing her stew, because she always adds the oregano at the very end. She says that we must always add the oregano at the very end, otherwise the oregano turns bitter. My father begins mumbling that he's going to cum all over me, that he'll cover my face with his tzatziki, when my mother screams from the kitchen: "Wait! Wait for me! Don't cum yet! I'll bring the trident!"

'I cry, "No, mummy! Please, not the trident!"'

The Voice with the long hair coughed, excused itself, and said: 'I don't understand. What do you mean by the trident?'

95

'It's a strap-on with three dildos attached,' Angie explained. 'You probably don't have such things in Egypt. Muslim countries are a bit behind in all that.'

'Have you ever been in a Muslim country?'

'I've only been to Sweden.'

'Then stop judging us, it hurts.'

'I'm sorry.'

'Never mind. Please continue.'

'So I beg my mother not to use her trident, but my mother laughs hysterically and jumps out of the kitchen dressed up as Poseidon, at the sight of which I faint.'

Angie took another good drag. She let the smoke rise slowly out of her mouth in curls. She remained silent and looked at the night sky.

'And then? What happened then?'

'Then I woke up in my bed and I was wet and I went for a swim to cool down. I didn't try to kill myself. I never knew that the Missing Sea was the most dangerous of all dangerous Seas. I was so lucky Missing Arm was around and saved me from those calamaries. Missing Arm is my saviour, my Prince Charming.'

'Yes, yes, he is,' said the Voice with the long hair. 'But this raping business must have been a horrible experience for you.'

'It's all right, I enjoyed it because it wasn't real. It was only a fantasy.'

'Then make sure next time you don't even put tomato on your father's souvlaki. That will make him really mad.'

'That's a good idea,' Angie said, and opened her legs. 'I'm so horny. And, you know, guys, I have a confession to make. I loved being watched.'

'We can only hear, I'm afraid. Would you like Missing Arm to finger-rape you?'

'Oh, no, no. I like the fantasy of being raped, the *fantasy*, but I'm a romantic really.' She turned and looked at the deserted beach, at the sea and the sky with the stars. 'We are on this mysterious, deserted island. It's so romantic here.'

Missing Arm pointed at the sky.

'Oh, yes, Missing Arm,' Angie said. 'Bright stars. It's such a beautiful night, my Prince Charming, my hero. I love nights like this one.'

'He's not pointing at the stars,' said the Voice. 'He's pointing at the moon.'

'There's no moon. What is he on about?'

'He's pointing at the missing moon.'

'How come you understand each other without talking?'

'That's what friends do.'

With that, Missing Arm clenched himself into a Superman-like fist.

'Watch him,' the Voice with the long hair instructed Angie.

Missing Arm rocketed off. He flew, bleeding his way flying to yet another world, and returned with the missing moon in his grip. He dunked the moon in the Missing Sea, brought it up and wrung it out. He returned to the beach and began washing Angie's body with it. It felt cool and soft and spongy, not rocky as they say. She opened her legs and Missing Arm washed away the confessed fantasies with the romance of the missing moon. He placed the missing moon under Angie's head and she closed her eyes with sweet tiredness.

The Voice with the long hair, who had remained silent for some time, now spoke: 'I will lullaby you with stories in my own language and you'll have the sweetest sleep.'

'That's so romantic,' Angie mumbled, turning onto her side. 'What stories?'

'The Arabian Nights. Original version.' And the Voice with the long hair began: *Alf Layla Wa Layla...*

Missing Arm caressed Angie's hair, waved goodbye to his friend, and crawled back into the water, where he belonged. He swam bleeding towards the heart of the Missing Sea, searching to save girls lost in bad dreams, swimming towards the end of this long long story.

In her sleep, Angie mumbled: 'I'll miss you, Missing Arm.'

3

It was dawn when Pavlo found a strange map behind the bar of Café Papaya. He had a look at it, and chucked it into the bin.

Sea-Worm

I spent the night waiting for the morning, trying not to forget. I took my diploma off the wall and fetched old documents from the drawers. Once everything was in my bag, I sat in the armchair and switched off the lamp, staying with the night. When the bell rang at 7am, I got into the taxi to come here.

This café was always my second home—it's by the harbour, for the poor lot. But I didn't change it even when I found the fishing village and struck gold. Nowadays, I come here every morning and try to remember. And every morning I tell my story to myself, imagining that people are living inside me and hear my story, and every morning more and more things are going missing. I can feel that; I've been struck three times. I'm scared now, scared to find out what's left of my story. But scared or not, I must crack on: bon voyage.

Let's see. I went to the sea when I was a nine-year-old kid. I was a deck-boy. That's the word, isn't it? Deck-boy. I don't know what you educated people call it. I became captain at sixteen. The best caïque-captain in Greece. Or maybe at fourteen. Can't remember. I think I was born in '29 and I became captain during the Greek civil war. You work it out. I don't want to confuse you.

Ah… I forgot to bring my bag. I'll bring it tomorrow, show you my diploma. And what a diploma, eh? Not a Mickey Mouse one. Twenty-five of us applied, only two got it. The others got shit. And, you know, everything is written properly on the diploma, scholarly-like. I was…

'Good morning, kyr Manolis.'

The waitress with the sweet smile. Every morning she saves this table in the corner for me. 'Good morning, my dear.'

'What can I get you?'

And she's a good worker, fast and slender, deer-like. 'I've forgotten your name, my girl. What's your name?'

'Angie.'

'Angie… Some milk, Angie.'

'Milk? Yes, of course.'

'With six…' Did I put on pomade this morning? 'Erm, six…' Wait, let me feel…

'Six sugars?'

Good, I did. 'Oh, no. Have you got…?' I always kept my hair short and tidy. 'I don't know how you call it.'

'Sweeteners?'

'No, no, no. Bread, crackers. That's it, crackers, a biscuit, something.'

'All right, I'll bring you some bread. Any sugar for the milk?'

'Six sugars. Good, well done.'

Right. So: I was the best caïque-captain in Greece. And I'm not ashamed to say so. Remember, Manolis Siderakis was the best seaman around. There's no one else. Say that the one and only and the best in fishing was found in this small town, in Kavala. His name is Manolis Siderakis—Manolis Siderakis, who became a captain at sixteen and ploughed the Aegean Sea with his caïque. Ah, I remember all that, but if you ask me, 'What did you do two days ago? Ten days, one month?' I won't remember.

Here, here. I'll show you some photos of mine. I always

carry them with me. In my wallet, in my back pocket. These photos are my sweet memories. I'll show you. Which one, which one... Ah, yes, this one, yes. Look at this one. I'm so young in this one. Hang on.

'Sweetheart. Girl. Come here a moment.'

Wait, wait, she's coming, you'll see.

'Yes, kyr Manolis.'

'Look at this photo of mine, sweetie. I'm so young here. Handsome, eh?'

'That's a phone-card, kyr Manolis. I'm too busy for this today.'

Yes, I always had a moustache. I look good here. So young. A young man who got his captain-diploma at sixteen. I've said that, didn't I? Pardon me, friends, if I repeat things sometimes. I worked hard—very hard—and after a few years, I strived to buy a small caïque. I excelled on that caïque, I made a good bundle of money, then I became partner in a bigger one. But it didn't work out. I was young and my partner stole, he mucked things up. So I worked hard again and I bought my own caïque. Thessalonica 147. Sixty tonnes. Engined trawl-net and trader. And before my twentieth birthday, I went out into the wide blue yonder, wealthy and good and a distinguished captain.

'Here's your milk, kyr Manolis.'

'Well done, my girl. What's your name again?'

'Angie.'

'Angie... Our eyes are the same colour. Did I tell you? Men with brown eyes are reassuring out at sea: it's the colour of soil, it's where you want to go back to when things get messy.'

'That's nice. And here you go. I'm afraid the bread is not very fresh, though.'

'Oh, it's fine, I like bread better when it goes hard. Thank you, sweetie.'

Good, a cup of warm milk and a story. Now let's leave the milk to cool down a bit.

Baedoz. Listen, listen, I remember! What a jackal I was, eh? Listen. During *baedoz*, the non-fishing weeks—we call them *baedoz*, I don't know if you've heard that before, that's the fishing term, *baedoz*—well, yes, during *baedoz*, other captains loafed around. But I'd look for more work. Eagled-eyed! I'd do everything. I'd pilot my caïque over to Thrace or to Thessaly—Thessaly: South-West of Salonica in case you didn't know—so I'd go there, load my caïque with watermelons and get them to all the islands. Even down to Rhodes. With my caïque. I would travel all around the Aegean. Lemnos, Mytilene, Chios, everywhere, everywhere. During *baedoz*, other captains went home to sleep. They'd go to bars and drink ouzo and whisky, but I was out there, on the sea, ferrying coal, olives, furniture, from the mainland to the islands, from one little island to another, fighting with the waves, but you know—well, how would you know?—it was a happy fight with the waves, they didn't scare me, the waves and the sea. For me the sea was like a mandarin. I'd peel it easily and eat it and it tasted good, fresh. I want to cry, cry, cry now, remembering all that...

'Girl! Waitress! Girl?'

'Yes, yes? What is it?'

'Thank you for the milk.'

'You're welcome. I hope it's not too sweet.'

'Of course not.'

Now, what else? Ah, yes. I'll tell you about my breakthrough. Captaincy and all that was good, but my breakthrough, what gave me loads of money and will go down in history because of me, because of Manolis Siderakis, is when I went down to Egypt. Listen, my friends. I'm an old man, and I'm ill, but I know what I'm talking about: go to every corner of Greece, go wherever there's a fishing harbour, and you'll find Egyptians working on the caïques. And that's because of me—it was I who started it. Listen.

Many, many years ago, how many I can't remember, I went down to Cairo. There had been a lack of fishermen here, Greek men had become lazy, they feared working at sea, and Greece and Egypt had signed a bilateral treaty, that's the word, *bilateral treaty*, I've got the papers at home, I'll bring them tomorrow, you'll see. As soon as I found out about that treaty, I said, 'That's it! I'm going down there to bring over *arapas*. I'll be the first!' People told me, 'How can you…? You're not good with the papers and words, how can you do all that?' They tried to stop me. But I started from here, Kavala. I went to many places that deal with paperwork, big buildings: City Council, Port Authorities, four or five places like that. I signed papers, went to lawyers. Then I took the airplane and went down to Piraeus. Piraeus, Athens. More papers and words and signatures and deals. More big buildings: Commercial Fishing Industry, Marine Ministry, Foreign Office. And imagine this: I was the first one in Greece who did all this and I only did four years in primary school. What a jackal, eh? Then I hired a translator, a lackey, and flew for Cairo.

Down in Cairo, I remember now. I remember I went down there the time when Cairo argued with another country. Do you remember when bombs went off and three hundred people died? I was there. It was hot, too hot. People were screaming and crying and the army was out and the tanks were in the streets. I didn't care what the devil was going on.

I went on with my business, visiting more big buildings and doing paperwork. In the end, at the Foreign Ministry, two officials took me to an office and offered me coffee and baklava and cigarettes.

'Mister Manolis Siderakis, well done. You've finished with the paperwork. Now you can get people to work up in Greece. How many would you like? One, two, three hundred? One thousand? We've got them ready for you.'

I sensed something was wrong, they made it feel too easy. And I didn't like it that they didn't use napkins and kept licking the baklava syrup off their fingers. 'Ready?'

'Yes. As many as you want.'

I didn't like them. Never trust men who eat baklava and smoke at the same time—you can't appreciate two pleasures simultaneously—they're the sort that muck things up. 'Where are they from?'

'Here.'

'From here?' I nudged the napkins towards them: '*Where* here?'

'From here. From Cairo.'

'I don't want them! There's no sea in Cairo. They aren't good sea-fishermen. I want good hands.'

'But we've got the Nile. They work the Nile.'

I didn't want them. Nile is a river, they say Nile is a God too, but I'm not scared of foreign Gods. We Greeks have St. Nikólas, the Sea Saint. I wanted men who knew the sea.

'I don't want them!'

'You don't want them? Then have a good day, Mister. Go find seamen yourself!'

I left their Foreign Ministry. Out on my own, I was in a foreign country, and war with the Jews was going on. I took my lackey with me.

'Come. Let's go to a café. Find me a big café where poor people go.'

We went to a café and I ordered tea for everyone.

'Listen!' I said to the people there, 'I want to find good fishermen. Fishermen who know the sea. Where is the best place to find these fishermen?'

Five or six men came to my table. 'Up North, but don't go there,' they said.

'North? Where North?'

'Where the Nile becomes the sea.'

It's easy to get facts from poor people, but you must be brutal to cut through their vagueness. 'And what's the name of this place?'

'It's a fishing village near Dumyat. It's the sea-eye of Egypt.'

'I don't care what it is. Tell me the name.'

'Ezbit El Burg, that's where the great sea-fishermen live.'

'And how far is this place?'

'Eight hours drive. Ten hours drive.'

'Order a taxi,' I said to my lackey. 'We're going to the fishing village right away!'

'Don't go,' they said, and grabbed onto my arm, 'the men there are strong and hateful. There are no hotels there, no decent place to stay.'

I shook them off, but I wasn't angry, they were trying to protect me. 'We'll find something.'

'Don't go! We are in war. There are rebels and thieves on the roads all along the way. You are a foreigner, they'll kidnap you, ask for ransom.'

We started driving North. I was fearless. Their roads were terrible, ancient, full of donkeys and camels and animal carts. Nothing happened on the way. Only that some men tried to stop us. They blocked the road, but they had no guns, only knives and axes and scythes. I threw a few notes at the driver and ordered him to keep on going: 'Drive fast. If they stay in the middle of the road, drive through them.' They made way, of course.

No foreigner had ever been in that place. Everything was dirty and filthy in the fishing village. Strong? The men were skin and bone. They were wearing these long dresses they have there, I don't remember what you call them, and they dragged them along in the dirt. There were four inches of filth on their dresses.

The women were all covered up in black robes, veils hid their faces, they even covered their hands with gloves in that terrible heat. The streets were full of rubbish, goats and dogs and cats and flies ate together from amongst the rubbish. The houses were pathetic, made of mudbrick. That's how I knew straightaway that many good fishermen lived there: only the fishing boats stood out. A thousand beautiful wooden caïques, with paintings on the hulls: eagles and eyes, the dark eyes of Arab women, big dark eyes with long eyelashes. I went inside to inspect some of them. They didn't have radars. No machinery. They were ages behind us Greeks. I picked a skeleton of a man and threw a bundle of old net at him.

'Mend it,' I said, and he took the needle from his pocket and worked on it. I nearly cried when I saw his craft.

I went in a café and all the fishermen came to me. Word had got around. *'Alkhawaga, Alkhawaga!'* They begged me to take them to Greece: *'Alhamdulillah! Alhamdulillah!'*

I drank their coffee and it tasted like mud. I spat it on the floor and ordered them to wait. I called one by one all the captains that I knew in Greece: 'Now, how many *arapas* d'you need? Five? Five costs so and so.' I gathered one or two hundred famished ones and packed them for Greece.

I made good money out of this. I didn't get money from the Egyptians. The deal was to get a cut from the Greek captains, but most of them didn't pay me all the money, and they stole from the Mohammedans, too. What sort of Christians were they, stealing from the poor? Go and listen to the stories of other captains if you like. Yes. Go. Go on. They'll lie to you. They are shit-mouthed. Out of all the captains, only five are the real thing. The rest are women-souled. Better forget that I've said this. I don't care, I'm ill—I want to be honest with you—but I don't want to ridicule the Greek captains. You'd better forget what I've just said.

So that was how it all started. During *baedoz*, I'd go down to Ezbit El Burg. In the beginning I staffed vessels with Arabs around Kavala (and without problems or prisons, because I've never been to prison, *others* have been). Then I spread my business throughout our lands, and for years, I sorted out all harbour-places in Greece. Salonica, Volos, Porto Lagos, Patra, Crete, everywhere, everywhere. And the Greek fishing industry flourished. Later, I stopped doing this. Other people smelled dough and went down there to do business, the path had been opened up by me. Right. Let me have my milk and bread now.

*

I want something in return for telling you my story. I want you to remember me. I want you to say that I was a capable man. Don't be sad about me. Never be sad about me. I'm old and ill, but I've still got the sea-worm inside me. And the sea-worm is alive, alive, alive. Alive and strong. So, now. Remember.

I had no problems with them Egyptians. As soon as I raised my hand, they bowed down. They bowed down to me like they did for their God, poor souls. How strange these Mohammedans were. Out at sea, at night, they washed their faces with sea-water, their hands and feet, they put a newspaper sheet on the deck and bowed to Allah. They prayed— how many times I saw the Mohammedans praying on the deck. And when St. Nikólas brought storms, when the storm brought high waves and it rained from the sky and the sea, their eyes searched in the raining darkness for their Mecca. They fell to their knees, brow on deck: 'Allahu Akbar Allahu Akbar.' I felt my heart cracking. 'Don't get angry with them, St. Nikólas, they were born in faraway lands, they have their own God, protect us all.'

No, I wasn't a bad man. Neither bad nor good. I was fair. If they dared to misbehave, I'd cast them back to Cairo. They were people who starved to death. And when you starve, you behave yourself. If they'd stayed in Egypt, they'd die of hunger. Hun-ger! Nobody should be hungry. I hope you never starve, friends.

I had to teach the *arapas* how to behave. When they first came here they were strays. I put them on a lead. Some of them forgot about their wives and went out with whores. And they learned to drink alcohol and gamble, that's why they're still broke. Those who worked on my caïque were quiet and harmless as sheep. Their families in Egypt wouldn't manage without me. Every time I went down there, their wives would bring me the few sweets they had and ask me, '*Alkhawaga,* what happened to our husbands? They don't come home. Why don't they come home? They spend the money over there and they don't come home.'

I'd say to the women, 'Don't worry. I'll sort your husbands out.' When I'd finish with my business there, I'd return to Greece and send the husbands back to Egypt to die of hunger. I was eagle-clawed. I acted with justice.

Never scared to be killed. Never scared to be beaten. At sea, the *arapas* did as I ordered. But, down in Egypt, they stole my wallet many times. One of my girlfriends down there used to steal from me, too. She was from some place, can't remember its name. She was married and had kids and her kids were starving. She used to steal from me, God rest her soul. I said, so what? I stole from no one. Get it? I owe to no one. I did everything with my own hands.

And now, so many years later, Egyptians from that village still work on our caïques. From grandfathers to their grandchildren. And I've heard stories that now all the men in that fishing village can speak Greek. Because they've all been to work here at some point. A whole village, a big village, thousands of *arapas* can speak Greek. That was because of me, remember, because of Manolis Siderakis, a fearless, brave man, a jackal who outstared all dangers.

'Girl! Waitress! Girl!'

'Yes, yes, coming, kyr Manolis, coming. What is it?'

'Tell me now, don't you think: "Fucking hell, how can this old man remember all this stuff?"'

'What stuff? Some more bread?'

What a lovely girl. 'No, thank you, my dear.'

So I did all these things in my life. I bought more caïques as the years passed by. I've travelled all around Europe on airplanes and ships. I've slept with the finest beauties. Me, Manolis Siderakis, who did four years in primary school. And I did many more things. Things that right up until my last days as captain only I could do. But slowly, slowly, I grew sluggish. And d'you know how they treated me in the end? I'm talking about the Greeks now. I'll tell you how they treated me.

It's the day of St. Nikólas the Sea Saint. I'm coming down here to the harbour church. I light a candle, and as I'm about to kiss St. Nikólas' icon, I'm struck down by something. I get up. Then it's St. Vasílis Day. I enter the church and I'm struck again. I get up. Epiphany comes. Me, as the president of fishermen, I gather everyone, all people—wealthy, poor, officials, the Bishop, all people—and we do the religious ceremony at the harbour. I believe you might have seen it, when we throw the crucifix into the sea. Later on, I put on a spread at the Fishermen's Society, where we cut the pie. So we have the dinner. I kind of fall asleep. They keep eating. I put on this spread for all those people for fifty years.

And that year, they knew I messed up. Once at St. Nikólas Day, once at St. Vasílis Day, they knew it, but they don't grab me to take me to the doctors or do anything. Whilst asleep, I hear my name: 'Manolis Siderakis will now cut the pie.' I do this, do that, until I manage to stand up. I go up the steps. Once I go to cut the pie, the thing strikes me for a third time. Nobody comes near me. I try to stand up, find the steps, get hold of the railings. I slip, legs first. They don't send for an ambulance. Nothing. I get up, make it home. Epiphany, a festive day. I make it to the door, open it. My family had a meal ready. A festive day.

TRUE BROMANCE

I t was early October, a dark evening. It had just rained and the café was empty. The phone rang and Pavlo answered it. It was his girlfriend. They talked. Then he hung up and went back to his barstool and looked at the deserted harbour. It was beautiful without people.

A fisherman came in, one who had recently returned from Ezbit El Burg. He was the Egyptian with the long hair. He stood by the bar and asked:

'You smoke?'

Pavlo nodded yes.

'Want smoke one with us?'

'Us?'

'Us. You. Me. Some other people.'

'Greeks?'

'No. Only you Greek.'

'Where?'

Long Hair pointed vaguely to the harbour.

'On the caïque?' Pavlo asked.

'Yeah.'

No. No, no. On the caïque he could be seen by anyone passing by. Maybe the Egyptians didn't care, their home was two seas away. But on the caïque Pavlo could be seen. 'We could smoke it below decks?' Pavlo asked.

'Yeah.'

No, no, no. Not a good idea. There might be people sleeping in the bunk beds. 'Look,' Pavlo said, 'you know, I don't want people to find out.'

Long Hair turned his back and walked away.

Maybe he didn't understand. Maybe after all those questions he didn't fancy sharing a smoke with Pavlo.

'Hey!' Pavlo shouted, and Long Hair stopped in his tracks. Pavlo said it hard, and straight, and out loud, the way foreign fishermen spoke: 'I want smoke with you.'

'Ah!' smiled Long Hair. 'I think you no want.'

And so, they arranged to meet at the café when Pavlo's shift finished at midnight.

Long Hair came along with One Arm. The waiter was pleased to see One Arm. He was one of his favourite fishermen. He always paid for his coffee, was always polite, never screamed when talking, never argued.

Somehow, One Arm managed to make a living. He lived with another seven or eight or ten fishermen, and spent his days and evenings and nights around the harbour: cafes, benches, walks along the seawall, calls from phone-boxes to his fiancée back home, visits to nearby hotels, sleeping with prostitutes.

One Arm, Long Hair, Pavlo. Midnight.

They walked off, towards the harbour.

The Egyptians were leading.

They passed by the caïques, when Pavlo asked, out of curiosity this time, where they would smoke. One Arm pointed to the far end of the harbour, towards the Port Authorities, where there were no streetlights, where it was completely dark.

They walked without talking much. They preferred it that way. All they could hear were seagulls squealing and caïques creaking.

On their left was the hill: the Old Town with its old houses, the fort with its walls, the Imaret with its curvy, pointed roofs, everything lit by orange streetlights. On their right: sea, caïques, moon, reflections.

They walked straight ahead.

One Arm said, 'You know, Pavlo, I want smoke with you for long time. Very, very, very long time. Since you gave your blood, when my arm was lost. But I am shy to ask you. I don't know you smoke hashish. I am very shy. I don't know how to ask you. So, I asked him to ask you,' and he pointed at Long Hair and laughed.

They all laughed.

'I am shy, too,' said Long Hair, 'but what can I do? He good friend for me. He said to me: "Please, please. Please go and find Pavlo. Ask him if he smokes hashish. Ask him if he want smoke with us."'

They were nearing the gate of the Port Authorities.

Someone in the distant darkness shouted: 'Hey! Where are *you* going to, eh?'

One Arm waved and shouted back, 'Hello there, my good friend!'

'Ah!' came the voice again, 'the lads from the caïques...'

They walked towards the voice, and there, next to the barrier, inside the cubicle, emerged the dim figure of a guard.

The old guard smiled.

They walked past the barrier.

There were ten two-storey buildings dotted around the grounds of the Port Authorities. Their walls smoky black. Windows all broken. Doors missing. Big trucks were parked everywhere. There must have been about fifty long trucks. All parked parallel to each other and so close that they formed alleyways, a kind of maze.

Pavlo walked through the maze with the Egyptians.

'There,' pointed One Arm. A shed amongst some buildings.

They stood under the roof of the shed, with the sea close by.

From somewhere up the Old Town, the street lamps cast bars of orange light into the dark sea. Night sea and strips of orange. Their eyes gazed at the orange sea-strips and their faces smiled.

Long Hair shoved his hand into the inside pocket of his jacket. Pulled out a pack of Marlboro, opened it. Slipped out a large, funnel-shaped spliff. An expertly rolled spliff. Put the pack back in his pocket. Got a lighter, stroked it, burnt off the spliff's excess paper. Pulled off the twisted bit. Gave the spliff to Pavlo.

'You want *me* to light it?' said Pavlo.

The Egyptians smiled. 'Yes,' they both said at once.

Pavlo lit it. Inhaled. Pushed it down to his lungs. Kept it there. Passed the spliff to Long Hair. Long Hair inhaled. Deeply. Pushed it down to his lungs. Kept it there. Passed the spliff to One Arm. One Arm shut his eyes. Inhaled. Pushed it down to his lungs. Kept it there. Kept his eyes shut.

Then the spliff went around every two puffs.

They talked about things that none of them would remember.

And they laughed. Giggled.

It began raining and it stopped raining. They felt cold. Zipped up their jackets.

'It's cold, but, you know, it's warm, too,' Pavlo said.

'Eh?'

'It's warm,' Pavlo said.

'What's warm?' One Arm asked.

'A manger is warm,' Pavlo said.

'A cunt is warm,' Long Hair said.

'Eh?'

'When we smoke,' said One Arm to Pavlo, 'we like to talk about women.'

Ah, women…

And what did Pavlo have to say about women?

He thought of his girlfriend. They'd been together since the Stone Age. She was the only woman he had ever slept with.

Is she pretty? Pavlo thought. *Yes, she's very pretty and sexy and she gives fine head.*

'Yeah yeah,' Long Hair said, 'we like talk about women. Yeah yeah.'

Shit, what am I supposed to say now? Is she romantic? Yes, she's romantic and so sweet.

The Egyptians looked at Pavlo. He had lit the spliff, now he had to begin talking about women.

Does she make me laugh? Yes, yes, she does make me laugh a lot.

'Yeah yeah. Women.'

She's pretty and sexy and romantic and she makes me laugh a lot. But, she's only one, only one woman. Shit. And what am I supposed to say?

They passed the spliff to Pavlo.

But Pavlo had nothing much to say about women. And as he had nothing much to say about women, he bit the spliff and took a long puff and said nothing about women. He only said:

'So no mangers, huh?'

'Eh?'

'Mangers.'

'Mange-whats?'

And so Pavlo said nothing about mangers.

And the Egyptians said nothing about women.

And they talked about things that none of them would remember.

The spliff ended. Pavlo looked down. How much he'd like to be able to talk with the Egyptians about women. Talk about women with them, like true friends.

But the cigarette had ended. Time to go back.

Ah, no, no, no.

The Egyptians stopped him.

One Arm gave a nod to Long Hair. Long Hair shoved his hand into his jacket. Pulled out the pack of Marlboro. Gave it to Pavlo.

'For you,' One Arm said.

Pavlo opened it. A large, funnel-shaped spliff. Expertly rolled.

'Take it with you,' One Arm said. 'Smoke it when you like.' He smiled.

Long Hair smiled.

Pavlo smiled too, but his smile was half a smile and half something else: 'If I take it with me, I'll have to smoke it on my own. Don't like smoking spliffs on my own. Let's smoke it together now. You want to?'

The Egyptians laughed. 'Yes, yes,' they said, and motioned to him.

'What?'

The Egyptians motioned to him again.

He laughed. 'You want *me* to light it *again*?'

Yes, they did.

Pavlo lit it. Sucked in. Hard. And so did Long Hair. And so did One Arm.

And for Pavlo's sake, they talked about things that none of them would remember. That's what they did. They talked about things that none of them would remember and it felt good.

'You know, Pavlo,' said One Arm, 'we also like after the smoke to go in a taverna and have a bite, and drink ouzo.'

'Good idea,' Pavlo said.

'Second best. After talking about women,' Long Hair said.

So they left for the only place open at that time, Café Papaya.

One Arm, Long Hair, Pavlo. Some time after midnight. They were walking back. No-one around. Just them.

They were walking, talking, laughing. Laughing, laughing, laughing.

And Pavlo wanted to become like them.

And he didn't think of his girlfriend.

And he decided that one day he was going to talk with them about women.

And now he thought of his girlfriend again. Not for long, though.

No. No, no. Oh no.

Because now he thought of that other girl with the wild lips.

Or the other one with the big, fat arse cheeks.

Hahaha.

Made by Sea and Wood, in Darkness

The harbour-side café was empty when a man in a Hawaiian shirt appeared from the darkness. In his fifties, in Bermuda shorts and flip flops, 'I knew your father,' the man said. 'Like you, he used to work night shifts here.'

The waiter looked at him. He was already looking at him, but now he had a proper look. And behind the man, beyond the seawall, he saw the lights of a caïque returning to the harbour.

'I just became a father,' the man spoke again, and the waiter moved his gaze back to him. 'Let's have a drink, young man. On me.'

He wanted whisky, and the waiter opened an orange Fanta for himself. They sat by a table near the open bar, under a lemon tree, and the man talked.

The caïque moored, the fishermen cleaned the nets and scattered into the night, except for one young, blond Egyptian who walked over to Café Papaya and asked for a Heineken. 'Bad catch. Problems with the engine.' He gave a nod to the man in the Hawaiian shirt, and sat a bit further away.

The man looked the immigrant up and down, and went on talking. He had been living in America for years now he said, and spent his summers on the opposite island, Thassos, where he owned a five star hotel. He earned so much money in America that he didn't bother about the hotel. 'I've got a yacht and just sail around. You know what? I'll take you for a trip. Let's sail the Aegean.' But what do yachts and hotels matter, the man suddenly threw his hands in the air,

what does anything matter now that his young wife had giv-
en birth? 'On my journey back from America I was so happy
that I forgot to declare the cash inside my suitcase. Can you
believe it?'

The waiter moved his eyes away from the man who knew
his father, and his gaze fell onto the Egyptian fisherman:
What's his name? He told me, I'm sure he told me before. '…
so the security at the airport in America they ask me: "How
much money are you carrying with you, sir?" "Whatever I've
got in my pockets," I say, "twenty-five thousand dollars."
"And the money in your suitcase? Did you declare that, sir?"
I say: "*Aman!* I've forgotten about it." They kept the money, seventy thousand dollars. "*Reh*," I tell them, "take it, *reh!*
Keep it." Of course. My wife was going to give birth and you
think I give a fuck for the bloody money? "Sure," I tell them,
"keep it as a tip for my baby's birth." Hahaha, what fuckers
these Americans…'

It seemed that the man had finished with his story, and
the waiter mentioned that he had to sort out the bar and
clean the coffee machine.

'Get me a whisky,' said the man. 'Ah… your father was
such a good man.'

A whisky was poured and served.

'Come, sit down, young man. Yeah, that's it, sit down.'

The waiter did so, but the man didn't talk now, he fiddled
with the glass, it seemed that something was playing on his
mind, and the waiter looked away.

'Look here. Here,' the man yanked his Hawaiian shirt. 'Do
you know how much this costs? Two hundred dollars. Now,
now… Can you guess how much I bought it for? Can you?
Go on, have a guess.'

The waiter only gave a faint smile.

'Tell me!' the man demanded. 'Have a guess.'

'I've no idea. How much?'

'Ten dollars. Yes, *ten*,' and he gulped down his whisky and threw the glass on to the marble table: 'Ten. Ten dollars. Do you take me for an idiot or what? Now, listen. The shirt is a top brand. I'm talking about high quality stuff. I can find this type of shirt very cheap in America and ship them over. All you need to do...'

He went on with the plan, while the waiter gazed towards the blond Egyptian.

It felt good looking at someone drinking his beer after a hard night's work, someone who was tired and needed that cool bottle. He had grown to recognise those who respected him as a waiter by the way they held the glass or the bottle, the knife and fork: there was no nerve in their grip, only tenderness, and a little melancholy. Rarely the locals showed any respect towards him. It was the Egyptian fishermen who had the kindness of the heart in their manners, the prostitutes and the spat-upon homosexuals, those beggars with a few coins to spend and those beggars whom the waiter loved and gave them for free the little they asked for. The customers he loved were the troubled ones, quiet, polite, and sparse with words usually; for them drinking was a ritual and the waiter part of that ritual, the one who served something that made sense: the bottle, a plate of food.

That voice wouldn't stop though, that voice that came out of that man who wore that Hawaiian shirt wouldn't stop, no, it kept going on, restless, feverish, foreverish, knocking on the waiter's skull with *plans*. He looked at the man's bright Hawaiian shirt and then he saw his own hand rising and hanging in mid-air. He didn't know why he had lifted his hand. The hand had lifted itself, and he felt like a schoolboy, an idiot. A finger pointed somewhere, and the glance of the man who knew his father fell upon the blond Egyptian, who smiled: 'Another beer, when you get a chance, Pavlo,' and Pavlo the waiter pushed his chair back and said, 'Excuse me.'

*

'I think you told me your name before, I'm sure you told me, but I can't remember it. Is it Mohammed?'

No, it wasn't Mohammed. The blond Egyptian fisherman said his name, but Pavlo instantly forgot it. He asked again, was told, and, once again, Pavlo forgot. Never mind. The Blond Egyptian.

They talked about the easy stuff, the shift in the café and the catch of the day.

'I like this time of the night. After every fishing voyage, I come here and have a couple of beers and look at the sea. I look at it thinking that one day I'll go back to my country. Back, to make a home, to get married and have kids. And I know that years later, when I do all that, I will like to sit in a café in my fishing village and look at the big Nile and remember the nights in Café Papaya.'

'I love nights, but nights without the people of my town. I never liked those, and I can't show them how I feel about it, I'm a waiter, you know, I must always be polite. Every time I go to take their order there is tension, they look down on me, they try to ridicule me and I can't understand why. I feel like a cornered rat. I did try to like them. For a period I used to work drunk to see if that helped with the situation and it didn't, I just got more wrecked by them.'

'After this beer I'll go and sleep in the caïque. You want to come and sleep there with us?'

The waiter stiffened suddenly, his face distorted. These words, this simple invitation shook him, and he fell silent: he felt comfortable with the Egyptian fishermen, he knew them, he knew that with them there was understanding, when he served them they were themselves and he was himself, and although he had never slept in a caïque before, he knew he'd have a beautiful sleep there. He wanted, he craved to go. Sea, wood and silence pulled him over, in the darkness of the harbour, into the hollow of the boat. And fear held him back. He didn't know why he felt like that, it was silly to be afraid, but the fear was there, raw and heavy, ordering him to stay put, guarding his words. He was so scared that he kept his mouth shut. He said nothing.

The Egyptian said nothing either, he didn't mention it again. They smoked, and again they talked about the easy stuff, life as a fisherman and life as a waiter, about Ezbit El Burg and Kavala.

Throughout this time Pavlo was thinking of the sleep in the caïque. He imagined the musty life below the deck, that smaller world under the hatchway. The gas lamp that would burn dimly, pouring its trembling light over bunk beds, blankets and wooden pillars. Light and shadow would play on the faces of the fishermen from Ezbit El Burg, revealing and hiding those deep hard lines on their cheeks and around their eyes, residues of their sorrows, carved by salt and wind on their sea voyages in the night. A hand would turn the wheel of the lamp and the sweet sounds of the darkness would take over, the slow creaking of wood in water, the dangling of brass lamps up on the deck, the sea. They would probably talk in the darkness—what would they talk about?—they'd talk until they'd all be too tired and their eyes would grow

heavy. And it was so close, so very close! No more than thirty steps away. Thirty steps, and he'd have a new sleep, the
most beautiful sleep, not a single soul in the world that dawn
would have slept better than him.

Pavlo didn't know where fears come from, how they take
over men and bar them from crossing streets, but he could
feel the fear, powerful in its filth, controlling, pulling his
imagination away from the caïque, dragging him back to dry,
secure land. *Back back back back, get me a whisky and look
at my shirt, I want my burger with cheese and without cheese,
where's my coffee, get me my coffee.* He spoke without thinking,
the words escaping from him, and they were simple words,
made by sea and wood, in darkness. He said he wanted to go
and sleep in the caïque.

The fisherman smiled. 'You want to come? Really? But I
forgotten, the mechanic will come soon to fix the engine. You
won't be able to sleep. Better come another time.'

It was time to go now. Soon it would be dawn. The Blond
Egyptian finished his beer and headed towards the caïque.
Pavlo the waiter got a brush and began sweeping the terrace
so that it would be nice and clean for the morning shift.

THE PHILANTHROPIST

They were supposed to meet in the café at 1pm. Petro arrived a little late and found the terrace empty. He chose a table in the shadow of a lemon tree and ordered his regular homemade sour cherry *vissinada*. He looked at the trawlers. He lit a cigarette and rested his eyes on the blue expanse.

They would come. He knew they'd come.

Petro was a well-intentioned man with sad eyes, who, when he was young he had worn his hair long so that it fell over his bright eyes. His smile was sweet, his manners were gentle.

The waiter brought his drink and Petro smiled, recollecting how he met three young Egyptian fishermen and that day they had invited him to the trawler's deck where they smoked apple-flavoured *nargileh* and ate those delicious *sukkary* dates. He found their company pleasant, and when they complained about their Greek captains and how unfairly they were treated, Petro patted them on the arm and spoke words of comfort. It seemed that he was the only Greek who talked with Egyptians and he knew well that the locals might regard him with a little concern for consorting with immigrants. But he did not mind, for he knew he was not like the others.

Petro was waiting for the three Egyptians, he would take them out for a meal in a traditional taverna. He planned to show them how Greeks enjoy themselves with plenty of food and alcohol. He wanted so much to show these immigrants a good time. He imagined himself talking about the traditional dishes he would order, what the ingredients were, how this and that dish were prepared. And, while daydreaming in this way, he felt a light hand rest on his shoulder.

'Sorry we're late,' said Ahmed. 'We finished work very late this morning. You been waiting long?'

'Please, don't stand like that,' Petro said. 'Please, take a seat.'

His Egyptian friends ordered coffee and lit cigarettes. Magdi began speaking about what everyone in the harbour was talking about these days. A fellow Egyptian, Rasool, had been caught by the police carrying drugs in his car-boot. They tried to figure out why Rasool might have done such a thing and who might have grassed him up. Mohammed said that it must have been someone from the Egyptian community, but Petro said he had his doubts about that, he couldn't believe that one of them would do such a thing.

Then the sad eyes of Petro saw a lonely Egyptian staring at them from across the harbour, an Egyptian with whom he had spoken a few times before and didn't like; Sayeed was his name. Many times he had seen Sayeed in the café speaking with undercover police officers. But this was not the main reason he disliked him. Sayeed was annoying because he talked too much and was always restless, so restless that he was always jiggling his knee.

Sayeed crossed the cobbled street and stood before them. They said their hellos, then Sayeed stood there doing nothing, just tapping his heel and chewing his gum, hands in pockets. Petro noticed his three friends withdraw their gaze from their countryman. Sayeed's eyes settled on Petro's.

'So what are you up to, guys?' Sayeed said.

His countrymen said nothing. Petro gave Sayeed the once-over. He didn't like this man, but it wasn't decent to leave him standing there, uninvited. 'We're thinking of going to a taverna,' he said, and, glancing at his friends, he saw them turn their eyes away. He felt as if his kindness was being tested. He slipped a cigarette out of his pack and stuck it between his lips: 'You coming?'

'Yes,' Sayeed replied, chewing his gum.

Petro couldn't sense any gratitude in Sayeed's answer, any recognition of his generosity in inviting him. He went for his lighter, wondering if inviting him was the right thing to do.

Sayeed's words came quickly: 'Why are you sitting like that then? Come on. Shall we go?'

Sayeed's words sounded to Petro more like an order than a suggestion. He saw the others standing up and he stood up too.

Sayeed spoke, 'I know a good taverna. A new one. In Old Town, opposite the Imaret. Want to go there?'

Before Petro had understood how plans had changed so quickly, they were all heading up, towards the hill, towards Kavala's Old Town and the taverna of *Al Khalili*.

*

In the taverna's small garden there was only one free table. Petro, who thought that his guests should have the better view, sat at the head of the table, facing the interior, and the others sat on either side. Next to him, on his left, sat Sayeed.

The waiter covered the dull-white cotton tablecloth with a paper one that, as he unfolded it, made a fresh, crisp sound. He wiped his sweaty brow with his thumb, and said that he would be back when they were ready to order.

'Wait a moment,' said Sayeed, and turned to his companions. 'Ouzo. Ouzo we gonna have, aren't we?'

'Let's take our time to decide,' said Petro. 'We're in no hurry.' He left his cigarette pack on the new tablecloth. On top of his pack he put his lighter. His friends did the same.

A drop of sweat trickled down from the waiter's temple, rested in the hollow of his sunken cheek. 'So you want ouzo or not?' he asked Petro.

'Look,' said Sayeed. 'Can you first bring us a jug of water? It's so hot.'

The waiter left and the only sound at the table was the sharp rolling of flint-wheels and the soft sound of burning paper around the tobacco.

Water jug and five tumblers were brought over, the waiter turned to leave.

'Hang on,' Sayeed stopped him. 'Can we have ouzo? Not from the barrel, bring us bottled Plomari,' and, looking at the others, he said, 'That's the best one.'

Petro saw his friends nodding with approval.

'Anything else?' asked the waiter, addressing Petro.

'Yes,' Sayeed replied instead. He poured water into everyone's glass and as he spoke his cigarette dangled in his lips: 'Bring us ice. Lots of ice.'

'Anything else?' asked the waiter again, still looking at the only local person at the table.

'No,' said Sayeed. 'Bring us the ouzo and then we'll let you know about food. Plomari, yeah? Not from the barrel.'

'Plomari all right,' said the waiter.

'Oh,' said Sayeed again, and pouring the last drops from the jug into Petro's glass, he handed the jug back to the waiter. 'And one more jug of water.'

When the waiter brought the bits and bobs, Petro took the bottle of ouzo, cracked it open, and poured some into everyone's glasses. Then he went for the ice-bowl. The ice-bowl was made from copper and Petro rested it on his hand, feeling its sweet metallic coolness along the lines of his palm, and asked whether they take ice with their ouzo.

'Of course we take ice. It's so hot,' said Sayeed.

'I guess it's much hotter in Egypt though, isn't it?' said Petro.

'Maybe it is, but I live here now.'

Petro dropped ice-cubes in everyone's ouzo, took the menu, browsed the list. Sayeed asked whether they were ready to order.

No-one answered.

'I suggest,' Sayeed said, tossing a glance around his companions, 'to have calamari and octopus. These two for sure. Now, what else?'

Petro saw his plans for the meal fall to pieces. He'd wanted to order dishes that the Egyptians had never tried before, but this immigrant wasn't giving him much chance. He didn't want to say anything to him though, as he might take it as an insult, and Petro didn't want that; he didn't like insulting people. So he looked at the menu and, as none of the Egyptians could read Greek, he began reading out loud the food on the list: 'So. Salads: beetroot with garlic, *melitzanosalata*, Greek sal–'

'We know, we know,' Sayeed interrupted him, and called for the waiter and gave his orders: 'All right. Two portions of deep-fried calamari rings, a portion of red-wined octopus...'

This immigrant was doing everything so fast—maybe because he was always so restless, Petro thought. He knew that

Sayeed's order would be the usual stuff, what the other three Egyptians had probably tried before. But he had planned to have a proper Greek meal, a *relaxed* meal, where he'd tell cooking stories while they ate and drank. But Sayeed was in charge now and no-one had challenged him yet.

'... two portions of fried anchovies,' continued Sayeed, 'two grilled chilli peppers, tzatziki, two portions of fries, a Greek salad, *taramosalata*, and... and what else? Ah, and grilled sardines. That's all, thanks.'

The waiter scribbled everything down on his order-pad and stubbed a full stop.

'And a portion of mussels *saganaki*,' interjected Petro, trying to gain some control over the food order. 'And a chilli cheese-cream.'

The waiter scribbled that, then lowered his order-pad and looked at Petro.

'And another bottle of ouzo,' said Sayeed. 'And more ice.'

More scribbling.

Then silence.

The waiter smiled. 'Anything else?'

'Nothing else,' Sayeed replied.

One by one, the dishes began to arrive and the five men began nibbling away. The ouzo went down much better now.

Petro didn't eat much. This meal was for the immigrants. They should have as much food as they fancied and enjoy themselves. A good time, that's what he wanted them to have. He was ready to ask them something about their country, maybe something about their families there—that would be a good subject to talk about, he thought—but as he opened his mouth, Sayeed leaned close to him and pointed at an antique wall-clock that was hanging on a pillar inside the taverna.

'Look at that clock, and look at the numbers. What kind of numbers are these? Do you know?'

Petro looked at the clock and the numbers on it. He was preparing to give his answer, when Sayeed said: 'The numbers on the clock are Arabic numbers.'

Petro looked at the numbers again and smiled to himself, thinking that Sayeed probably hadn't even finished primary school back in his own country. Then he recalled that just behind his back was the Imaret, the old, beautiful Egyptian building. He knew all about the Imaret—two hundred years ago it was presented to the citizens of Kavala as a gift of love and power by Mehmet Ali, the man that was born in this town when it was still under Ottoman rule, and who went on to become the founder of modern Egypt, and its king. But Petro said nothing about it. Instead, he told his companions that the name of this taverna, the *Al Khalili*, was taken from the title of a popular Greek song. Ahmed said that *Khan Al Khalili* was actually a huge open-market back in Qahera, as he called Cairo, and Mohammed added that the mussels *saganaki* that Petro had ordered were a very good choice.

They ordered more bottles of ouzo and Petro felt his ears burning and knew that his cheeks must now be red. This worried him. He looked at the faces of the Egyptians. Their cheeks were a bit red too, and he liked that, it made him feel better, less worried. And as he was looking at them he realised that he had not said a word for some time and that his companions were not speaking in their broken Greek any more.

Left alone, Petro didn't know what to do. He drank and refilled his glass, stole glances at Sayeed's jiggling heel, drank more, looked at his belly. He had a big belly and was ashamed of it. Bitterness rose in his throat. He looked up: Sayeed was saying something to the others in their language, it seemed like he was telling a story. Too much ouzo without food made Petro's mouth go dry and numb. He took a long breath. The air made him feel better and he took another long breath. He realised how hungry he was. He glanced at the Greek salad… He wished he was all alone so that he could break off a hunk of crusty bread, dab it in the salad's juices, and cram it into his hungry, hungry mouth. But he couldn't behave like that in public, it wasn't decent. So he scooped some tzatziki and ate it. But the tzatziki had been in the sun for too long and tasted horrible. He knocked back his ouzo to wash down the bad taste. His belly ached. He slipped his hand under the table, unhooked the belt and popped open the top button. He sat back, sighed, smoothed his few hairs back, and remembered a time he had long hair and was young and strong and had dreams and wanted to meet lots of women and be a great lover, maybe the greatest lover ever. He liked remembering all that, although the memories made his throat feel hard and choked-up. He drank more—without ice, he couldn't be bothered reaching out for the ice-bowl. An irritating noise came from under the table, Sayeed's jiggling knee brushing against the table leg. He kept his eyes on the table and heard them all speaking in Arabic, they went on and on, and this foreign language gave him a headache and he felt so annoyed he had to close his eyes to shut everything off.

'Excuse us for talking in Arabic,' said Magdi. 'You must get bored.'

'Please, don't worry about it. I'd probably do the same if I were you.' Talking revived him. 'I don't mind. I don't mind staying silent. I like it. Many times I stay silent like that.'

'What were you thinking about?' one of his other friends, Ahmed, asked.

'Ah… Many things. Past things. The time I was young.'

'How old are you?' Sayeed asked.

'I'm fifty-one,' Petro said. 'And you?'

'How old you think I am?'

'Don't know. Twenty-seven or so?'

'Thirty-four.'

Petro took guesses about the age of the other Egyptians; he always got it wrong. Ahmed, Magdi, and Mohammed liked this sort of game and they laughed and Petro felt good.

Sayeed didn't laugh. 'You look much older,' he said to Petro.

'Do I?' said Petro, and listened to the annoying immigrant saying that Petro looked much older because he was very stressed, and that he had problems and should avoid any kind of hassle and take some rest.

Instead of an answer, Petro turned his eyes on Sayeed's jiggling heel. He wanted in this way to show him who really was stressed, but soon he realised that that was too subtle a hint for the rough immigrant to grasp.

Sayeed didn't move his eyes from Petro: 'Don't think too much. Thinking much is no good. You see how much younger we look? That's because we have no problems. The only thing that I care about is fucking. And that's why I fuck so good. Not only me. All the Egyptians who live here.'

Petro felt his blood coursing through his veins and when he spoke he didn't care about manners and his eyes weren't sad any more. 'You may fuck well. But we may fuck well too. Got it?'

Sayeed's face turned serious, thoughtful, almost respectful. He turned to his countrymen and said something in Arabic.

Petro stayed silent, knowing that he now hated the immigrant. For he might be a gentleman, but gentlemen don't have to swallow every insult. No, he wouldn't tolerate this annoying man's behaviour any more. His hands trembled from the suppressed anger as he poured ouzo into his glass. He knocked it back, half of it gushed out of his mouth and stained his shirt. He checked to see if the others had noticed. They hadn't. They spoke in Arabic again. He checked to see if any other customers had noticed. There were no other customers... How long had they been in the taverna? The garden wasn't bathed in bright sunlight any more. The sun had moved lower, behind the Imaret. The old Egyptian building had the garden under the control of its shadow now. The interior of the taverna was even darker. And there, in the darkness, Petro's eyes met with the waiter's, who puffed on his cigarette and grinned: 'Anything else?'

Petro felt for his glass of water, found it, gulped it down. He swept his brow and remembered that he wanted to say something and make Sayeed shut up. But he didn't know what to say and the shadow of that building behind him felt heavy, so heavy that his shoulders shrank, and as no-one was paying him attention anyway, Petro said nothing.

And then suddenly he realised how to gain back his friends' respect, to confront Sayeed's continuous and unfair attacks, to turn defeat into victory.

The Egyptians were still speaking in their language. They seemed to be in deep conversation. But Petro was determined. It was his last chance. With a strong voice that broke their conversation, he said, 'We must help Rasool.' Looking not at the men, but at his ouzo, he said louder, 'We must help him.'

The Egyptians stopped talking and, at last, there was silence.

And Petro the philanthropist repeated: 'We must help him. We must do something for him.'

His three friends expected Petro to go on. He knew that they *wanted* him to go on. But Petro didn't go on. He let his head hang down over his ouzo—but that was part of the plan he had devised, he wanted them to believe he had no strength left; he felt like an insect, pretending to be dead.

Magdi said that what Rasool had done was really bad and that selling drugs was a crime. Mohammed and Ahmed agreed.

And then, when no-one expected him to say any more, Petro raised his head: 'Doesn't matter.' He looked up at his three friends, clearly ignoring the one he hated, and declared triumphantly: 'We all make mistakes sometimes. Different kinds of mistakes. It's the forgiving that matters.'

Ahmed nodded thoughtfully. Magdi and Mohammed looked at Petro with respect.

Petro went on. 'Boys, we shouldn't leave Rasool on his own in the prison. It's not right.'

'You are right, Petro,' said Sayeed. 'First we need to find out what's going on with Rasool.'

Petro wondered what Sayeed was playing at. If only he wanted to help... it would mean he was acknowledging his mistakes, and that's all Petro wanted, just a small, tiny gesture, and he would have forgotten and forgiven everything, everything. 'We must get some money together for Rasool,' Petro said. 'If we all give something, he could find a good lawyer. There are a hundred Egyptians in this town. If everyone could give someth-'

'Right,' Sayeed cut him short, and turned to the others: 'What do we do now, guys? It's getting late. Shall we make a move?'

Magdi, Ahmed, and Mohammed agreed. It was time to get going. But none except Sayeed seemed to be in any hurry. Sayeed insisted and signalled for the bill. 'I got things to do,' he said, 'we should get going.'

The bill was brought and Petro paid. No tip for the waiter.

The Egyptians stood up, Petro remained seated.

'Are you all right, Petro?' Ahmed asked.

'Hang on,' Petro said. He slipped his hand under the table and buttoned himself up.

On the way back to the harbour Sayeed was walking fast, talking on the phone in Greek. The rest followed him. While Petro was trying to persuade the others to help the drug dealer, he overheard Sayeed and he knew that he was talking with a woman.

When they reached the harbour, Sayeed was already further ahead of them. The rest shook hands and said goodbye.

Petro got into a taxi.

His three friends climbed onto their trawler.

Sayeed kept walking far down the quay.

*

Petro got out of the taxi. He stood, facing his front door. He entered and closed the door behind him.

His home was empty.

He went into the kitchen, opened the fridge, got out a packet of ham, and ate one slice after the other until the packet was empty. His eyes fell on a jar of chocolate spread. He ate that too.

He lay on the sofa, looked around. Everything was in the right place, tidy. He sighed. His brow was sweaty. He dried it with his palm and smoothed his few hairs back. And then he remembered a time when he had long hair and was young and strong and had dreams and wanted to meet lots of women and be a great lover, maybe the greatest lover ever.

He found the heat annoying and unbuttoned his shirt.

But that wasn't enough.

He took off his shoes and trousers.

No, that wasn't enough.

He took off his socks and underwear.

Not enough.

He began masturbating, his throat hard and choked from remembering, he finished, and reached out for a tissue.

SCABABIAS

THE MAGIC ALLEY

Fifteen or so boys settled about the water-taps area and gazed at him: in the playground's corner, squatting on his big rock, Scababias had his back towards them. A boy made a signal and a team of three gathered stones, walked on tiptoe, took cover behind a bush: not far from him, not too near.

A lizard popped up from under a stone, and Scababias hawked up phlegm. His eyes narrowed and focused on the little creeper, and he parted his lips slowly, revealing the gap between his front upper teeth. The lizard cocked its head towards him, and he shot his spit through the gap teeth: the serpent disappeared back into its hole.

'Hold fire,' whispered one boy.

Scababias remained in squatting position, utterly motionless, insect-like.

'Why not stone him?'

'Only if he attacks us.'

They waited.

He waited.

'Enough. Let's go back.'

They crawled back and joined the others by the water-taps, gave their report: 'His spitting ability is scary.' 'He's dangerous.' 'What if he spits on us?'

The kids agreed that they weren't happy with Scababias's exile. It seemed that their plan to banish him to the playground's corner hadn't worked as they had wished. In his solitary confinement, inspired by hatred and boredom, Scababias had been working on his saliva, shooting his spit at various targets with accuracy, scaring off his schoolmates, turning his place of exile into his own land, his kingdom.

'We must find out what he is up to.' 'Let's check him out through the dark alley.' 'I'm not going.' 'I'm not going.' 'I'm not going.' 'You go.' 'No, you go.' 'How about the lonesome hero?' and they looked at the boy who sat on the floor, away from them, Pavlo.

Pavlo stood up and walked off.

'Pavlo... Don't you need help?'

'I work better alone.'

'No back up?'

'Your prayers and thoughts are my back up.'

He headed towards the alley, a narrow passage that ran parallel with the back of the school building and a high wall that separated the playground from the residential area. The alley was abandoned and, even on shiny mornings, dark: the trees which stood on the other side of the wall provided a natural roof. It was a tunnel that led to the heart of Scababias's kingdom. None of the other kids dared to enter there, scared off by the idea of sharing darkness with Scababias, and the stories Pavlo told them about the exiled boy's behaviour in there.

Pavlo stood, the daydarkness in front of him, and he walked into it. Slowly. The upper coat of the soil was a thick and soft mud, like chocolate spread, sweet squelchy sounds echoed as he made his way forward, and the birdsong from outside vibrated more melodic, more and more melodic as he penetrated the heart of daydarkness. He turned, looked back at the place where he was standing earlier: it was bathed in light. Now that his eyes had adjusted to the darkness, he could see around him, but no-one could see him from outside. It was his magic alley, a sense of home.

He walked amongst cobwebs and bugs and strange plants that grew in darkness, his eyes and hands searching, carefully searching for more magic. He found the place where some bricks protruded a little. Using the bricks as steps, he climbed up the wall and sat on the ledge with his back to the school, hidden in the foliage of the oak tree. Through the branches, he looked at the house opposite: the curtains in the kitchen were drawn open, a big pot was simmering on one of the hobs. There was no-one there, though, and he didn't have much time. As he was about to climb back down, he noticed movement in the kitchen. Ah, there she was… The housewife with the big bum. With his foot he pushed away a branch to get a better view. She put on her apron. God, she was going to cook. Pavlo unzipped his trousers: now she opened the oven door and bent over to check the pie… now she got a long wooden spoon and lifted the pot's lid to give it a stir, to take a whiff of the rising steam… What was she cooking there? Was it okra again? Pavlo finished masturbating and climbed down.

He walked to the other end of the alley and watched the bony Scababias squatting: he looked like a mosquito. He stepped out into the light; Scababias spotted him and walked slowly towards him.

The boys by the water-taps screamed: 'Pavlo! He's coming.' 'Pavlo, careful!' *Pavlo, Pavlo, Pavlo…* He wished they would shut up, the cowards. He picked up a stone and drew a line in the mud. Scababias squatted in front of the line, looked up at Pavlo. Pavlo scanned his surroundings. A big spider, motionless for a long time, must have sensed Scababias's presence and disappeared into a hole. Scababias pulled something from his pocket and gave it to Pavlo. A battered cigarette, a lighter. Pavlo cleaned them in his t-shirt. He smoked a bit, passed it back, pulled out a torn page from a porn magazine, gave it to Scababias: 'Your homework.'

The two boys smiled at each other.

Then Pavlo walked back and joined the others out in the light.

'What happened, Pavlo?' 'Are you injured?' 'Shall we call the medics?'

'Listen, don't you ever go inside the alley.'

'What did he do to you?' 'Did you see him?' 'Did he harm you?'

'I was hiding. He couldn't see me. But I saw him.'

'What was he doing?'

'He was jerking off again...'

'Oh, how disgusting. You're so brave to enter the alley.'

'Don't mention it, guys.'

'You are a true hero.'

Back in the classroom, Scababias wasn't a big threat to anyone. Naturally, no-one wanted to share a desk with him. His desk was right at the back, in the corner. The two desks in front of him and the two on the other side were vacant— what the pupils referred to as the safety zone.

'Why does nobody sit near Scababias?' the teacher had asked them.

'Doctor's orders,' the students had said, and the teacher couldn't hide his smile.

The teacher turned a blind eye to all that. He understood them all, they were just kids. To make up to Scababias, he never tested him on the lessons and left him in peace. And Scababias spent his time in the classroom quietly. It was only when the kids harassed him that he would react by grabbing his genitals.

*

About thirty pupils, boys and girls, gathered around the water-taps area to discuss burning issues regarding Scababias. The team that observed Scababias's exile reported that the boy's behaviour was worsening. Whenever they visited his corner to spy on him, they would come back terrified by his vicious spitting skills which they were certain he would use for his revenge. At the alley front, the lone patroller, Pavlo, kept feeding reports about Scababias masturbating in the darkness, rendering the alley completely off-limits. On top of all that, recently Scababias's toothless, crazy mum had neglected to shave her boy's head once a week and, as a result, his nits 'could take off anytime from his dirty head and, like tiny helicopters, land in ours,' as a fat little boy put it.

The situation was getting out of hand. Stricter measures should be taken.

The leaders asked for suggestions on how to further restrict the boy.

'Let's stone him!' 'Yes, let's stone him every day!'
YES! YES! YES!

And they would have stoned him if the leaders hadn't talked them out of it: 'Violence must be our last resort, people. We mustn't stone him, unless we have to defend ourselves.'

Once everyone had calmed down, three girls announced that they had seen Scababias many times licking his own bogeys off his finger.

'How come I never saw him doing that?' said Pavlo.

'Girls have an eye for details,' said another boy. 'It must be true.'

'It's not true,' said Pavlo. 'Scababias never does that. The girls are lying.'

'Why is Scababias the way he is?' asked someone.

They fell quiet for a short while, contemplating.

'He's a leper,' a boy said.

'A leper?' 'A leper, a leper.' 'Look at him, he must be a leper.'

They all turned and looked at the corner, where Scababias was squatting on his big rock, as usual, only this time he was staring back at them.

'Leprosy is a contagious disease,' said a girl.

'YOU ARE A LEPER, SCABABIAS.'

Scababias grabbed his genitals.

'Look at the bastard!' 'Let's go and stone the leper!' 'Stone the leper!'

YES! YES! YES!

They began gathering stones.Even the leaders picked up stones: 'We have no other choice, people. He's dangerous.'

They headed towards his place of exile, they were going to do it.

'Wait, wait…' said Pavlo from his corner. 'Don't stone him. That would be too much for the teachers.'

'Who cares. Let's stone the leper!'

'WE COME TO STONE YOU, SCABALEPER.'

Pavlo stood up. 'There's no need to stone him. He's not a leper.'

'And who are you to tell us what Scababias is?' said one.

'Who am I?'

'Yes. Who are you?'

'I am the lonesome hero of the dark alley.'

Quickly the leaders informed the crowd that Pavlo was indeed the hero of the dark alley; they even told of a few of his adventures in the darkness, and everyone looked at him in awe.

'He's not a leper,' Pavlo said. 'Don't stone him.'

'Then what is it, Pavlo?' 'Tell us what you think, dark hero.'

'He's nuts. But if you think he's a leper, there's something else you can do about it.'

They decided to follow Pavlo's suggestion for a peaceful solution: they wouldn't stone him, but in order to protect themselves from leprosy, an additional sanction was imposed on Scababias. They appointed one of the water-taps (the one next to the toilet's entrance that wasn't working properly) as Scababias's personal tap. He wasn't allowed to use any other taps. For hygiene reasons, they made a sign out of cardboard that read,

DANGER

LEPROSY

STAY AWAY!

...and hung it above Scababias's tap.

They spread the news quickly. And, before the bell rang for the last time that day, everyone in the school had been informed that Scababias was a leper, including the boy himself.

Pavlo carried on with the mission of patrolling the dark alley, and after each time he finished masturbating, he drew a line and had a smoke with Scababias.

So one day, when Pavlo was hanging around the third floor balcony with some other students and heard someone screaming, 'The thing is here! It's angry!' he didn't worry, he was his secret friend after all.

'Why aren't you in your corner?' a boy asked Scababias.

Scababias grunted.

Someone shouted: 'The time has come! He's here for his revenge!'

RUN FOR YOUR LIVES.

Pavlo's friends hurried into a classroom and barricaded the door by pushing desks against it. Everyone but Pavlo disappeared, and Scababias advanced slowly, smiling at the only available prey.

'Run!' screamed a girl who was watching from a classroom window. 'What are you waiting for? *Run!*'

'Could it be…' thought Pavlo, and locked eyes with Scababias, who licked his lips softly. Oh, no… Pavlo beat it towards the stairs, looked back: Scababias was running after him. He jumped down the steps in threes: 'But we're mates, Scababias!' He turned back and saw Scababias jumping down the steps in threes, too. 'Bugger…' Another flight of stairs, Pavlo reached the bottom, turned back: Scababias was jumping in fours. 'Oh, God…' He shot down the last flight of stairs and reached the playground. He felt better now, with all his mates around him… He relaxed his run into a light jog. Some students said hi and some asked him if he was in a hurry, but when they saw Scababias running after him, they began screaming and ran away.

'Where are you going?' Pavlo asked them. 'Get stones… Stone him!'

They didn't get stones. They just moved away.

Now only the two were running, the others watching.

A boy from up a balcony shouted: 'There's no way he can escape Scababias!'

A girl from another balcony shouted back: 'He can do it. He's the lonesome hero of the dark alley!'

'The alley,' Pavlo thought, 'I have to make it there and draw a line.' In his panic, he headed the quick way, towards the boy's kingdom.

Scababias laughed out loud. No-one had ever heard him laughing.

'Hey, Scababias, you scare me, mate...'

Heeeeee-hee-hee-hee.

Knees pumping, Pavlo entered the abandoned kingdom, saw the entrance to the magic alley, took off for it. He would be safe there somehow, no-one could harm him there. But then he felt Scababias's filthy fingers touching his clean arm, and his knees shook. He elbowed him and ran quicker.

Hee-hee-hee...

Pavlo entered the darkness, fell to his knees, quickly cleaned his elbow with his t-shirt, looked for a stone. But it was too late to draw a line now: he felt Scababias's hot breath on the back of his neck. He looked up towards the other end of the alley, where there was light. A little blond girl with pig tails was sitting on the soil, playing with a flower, free, safe.

'Get up,' Scababias whispered in his ear.

He got up, turned around: the boy was smiling, knowing that now, at last, there were no lines, only freedom to do as he pleased.

'I always tell the others what a nice guy you are, Scababias.'

With a long, dragging sound, Scababias gathered spit in his mouth.

'No no no no. The leprosy stuff have nothing to do with me. Scababias, I have influence. I can persuade them to put an end to your exile.'

Scababias parted his lips, showing off the gap between his front teeth, from where saliva was oozing out.

'Wait, wait. Would you like to see the housewife?'

He spat down on to the mud. 'What housewife?'

'Come...' Pavlo found the steps on the wall and climbed up, Scababias following closely. They sat side by side on the ledge. Luckily, the housewife was in the garden, hanging clothes on the washing line.

'You like?'

Scababias scratched some yellow gum from the corner of his eye.

'Ah good, you can see better now... Look, look...'

The boy examined the yellow gum instead.

'You know, you don't have to eat it, Scababias.' He offered him a leaf and Scababias wiped off the gum.

'Look at her... Look how beautiful she is. Let's do our homework.'

Scababias dragged up saliva and made to spit at the woman, but Pavlo reached out his hand and blocked Scababias's mouth: 'Not her. Please, Scababias, don't spit at her. Let's get back down and you can spit on me.'

They climbed down and stood opposite each other. A ray of sun penetrated through the leaves and played on Scababias's face. He hawked up phlegm.

Pavlo nodded behind him, towards the light: 'Scababias, mate, look at that lovely blond girl. Wouldn't you like to spit at her instead?'

He shook his head.

The ray of sun hit Scababias in the eyes and Pavlo made to beat it, but the squelching sound of his footsteps on the mud gave him away, and Scababias sneered down at him. Then the exiled boy moved his head up and stared straight back at that sunray—and spat at it. His phlegm went through the gap on the leaves, and, for that one moment, it blocked out the sun.

He looked at Pavlo, smiled, and ran past him, towards the end of the alley. Once the little blond girl realised who was coming towards her, she cried out for her mummy.

The boy, without stopping, screamed at her: 'I'm Scababias!'

And disappeared out into the bright light.

THE MAGIC CURRANT-BREAD

At 8am Pavlo finished his night shift at Café Papaya, and stepped out of that place, soul-beaten. He breathed in the cold winter air, reclaiming hope. He didn't like his townsfolk, he couldn't like them, he had tried. The streets of his town of Kavala were wet. He wasn't in the mood to stroll by the harbour as he usually did, and he dragged his way towards the town centre. He avoided meeting the eyes of the locals, they didn't like him. There was something wrong with him, he thought, as he walked the streets. 'Or there's something wrong with them. It's either them or me.' And he walked, he walked keeping his eyes low, defeated by the many. He saw a bookshop, its window covered in posters with writers' quotes. He stopped there, rolled a cigarette, and smoked it while reading the quotes one by one. None struck him. He walked off.

A bakery around the corner, another bakery, another bakery, another one: no, this one was different, not like all those bakeries with their windows stuffed with loaves of bread and *tsourekia* and pies that looked perfect and shiny, fake and plastic. This bakery drew his attention: old and decadent, its windows were empty. Above the entrance, a weathered wooden sign that hung from two chains read: *THE MAGIC YEAST*, and below, in smaller letters: *fresh currant-breads*. Pavlo peeped inside: it was empty. He went in.

The floor was made of black and white square tiles, chess-like. At the back there was a wooden table with currant-breads, behind which stood the baker, a big man with a bushy beard: 'GOOD MORNING, SIR! WHAT CAN I GET YOU, SIR?'

Pavlo looked behind him. He turned to the baker. 'You talking to me?'

'YES, SIR! WHAT CAN I GET YOU, SIR?'

'Do you make coffees?'

'AY AY, SIR!'

'Why do you shout at me, man?'

'HOW WOULD YOU LIKE YOUR COFFEE, SIR?'

'BLACK. TWO SUGARS.'

'ALL RIGHT, SIR!'

He sat down at a table in front of the window, in a corner, and didn't take off his jacket. The street outside was busy, full of the locals he disliked. He wished it was empty.

'HERE'S YOUR COFFEE, SIR!'

'Eh, listen. I'm not a lieutenant. Please don't shout at me.'

'All right. Now *you* listen to me, young man… You come to a bakery and ask for coffee. Are you thick or what?'

'That's none of your business.'

'Do you want a currant-bread for free?'

'No, I don't.'

'I'll give you one anyway. And you'll eat it.'

'What, you'll make me eat it against my will?'

The baker picked one out, returned to Pavlo.

'If you try anything with this, I'll inform the authorities.'

'Ooooh...' exclaimed the baker, pressing the little bread in his fingers. 'Feel how soft it is... So fresh. Fresh and soft like the flesh of innocent little girls...'

'Do you fancy children, then?'

'Oh yeah... Don't you?'

'I prefer their mums. Take this thing away from me. I don't want it.'

The baker returned behind his currant-breads, and Pavlo gazed out towards the street, and drank coffee: it was tea. He pushed it away. An old man entered the bakery. An old man in a beautiful black overcoat, resting his trembling hand on his cane's golden knob. Hunchbacked and bald, his lips were sunken the way toothless people's lips sink into their mouths.

'HELLO!' boomed the baker.

'Me-moo...' the old man said.

'Me-moo...' the baker imitated. 'What's that? Me-moo?'

The old man sat down at the table in the other corner. He didn't take off his coat.

The baker walked over. 'What you want?'

'A bamby.'

'A bamby, eh? What's a bamby? Come again, arsehole?'

'Bamby.'

'Ah, brandy... Pay me.'

The old man gave him a few coins: 'Fenkf.'

'Don't thank me yet. Give me the money you owe me from last week, Betty...'

'I bave vem laft veek.'

'No, you didn't. Now pay me or I'll break your fingers.'

The old man gave him a few more coins.

'And a few more for a currant-bread,' said the baker. 'Or will you refuse my marvellous currant-breads, Betty...?'

The old man gave more coins.

'Fenkf,' the baker imitated him, went back to the counter and, grabbing the bottle of brandy from the shelf, he called to Pavlo: 'You know him? He's an old poof.'

Pavlo looked at the old man. He didn't react, he was gazing out into the street.

'Nah, don't you worry about him,' the baker said. 'He's almost deaf, he can't hear us.' After some consideration, he picked a currant-bread from the very end of the flour-dusted table, and served the old man. 'So you don't know him?' he said as he approached Pavlo and sat by his table. 'Look at him. He's got no teeth left. The bloody old faggot. He's a famous arse bandit, you know.'

'Why you sit at my table?'

'He's gay, homosexual, I don't know what you young people call them.'

'I don't care if he's your aunty. Get away from my table.'

'Oh, you don't care... I wonder why's that...'

'I don't care what you do with little girls either.'

'Once upon a time he had a lot of money.'

'Piss off or I'll tell the police that you fuck kids.'

'The best tailor in town he was, back when Kavala was wealthy from the tobacco factories. He used to clothe the factories owners' wives who lit their cigars with 5,000 drachmas notes. People said that he was offered work in America.'

'At least can you get straight to the point?'

'Are you upset, young man? I wonder what puts you so on edge...'

'You drag it out. Something happened and he lost everything. So what was that?'

'He spent all his money on boys. On young boys.'

'Some people like young boys, others like little girls... Personally, I'm into mums.'

'Everything's gone now. His money, the apartments, the shops, everything. Look at him.'

They both turned towards the old man.

'He can't even eat. I gave him a hard stale currant-bread on purpose. And believe it or not, young man, he's still after boys. Everything he spends on boys. Who the fuck would go to bed with him? Bloody disgusting...'

Dark clouds invaded the sky, it began raining. Now it felt good being in that old little bakery. Pavlo looked at the old man, checked him out for signs of arrogance, couldn't spot any. He looked like a good, humble old man, troubled. The old man took the stale currant-bread in his hands; the crust broke and some bits fell down onto his black coat. He placed it back on the plate and looked at it. He stayed like that for some time, doing nothing, just looking at the little bread that he couldn't eat, until he took it again in his trembling hands and managed to tear away a chunk. He kissed it, and dipped it in his brandy, softening it. His whole face was moving as he chewed it with his gums. Once he swallowed it, his eyes opened widely, as if the little bread had brought him back to life.

The rain fell hard, a storm. Raindrops dribbled down the bakery's window, and the empty street looked different now, clean. A motocross bike streaked along the wet street and slammed on the brakes in front of the bakery. It revved up, its exhaust drowned out the sound of the storm. The rider got off, removed his helmet. He was young, of medium height, long brown hair fell on the sides of his pale face, partly covering his eyes. He pulled his hair back and Pavlo felt a chill run down his spine. He looked at him more closely. It was Scababias.

He entered the bakery.

'Wipe your feet,' said the baker, and Scababias gave him the eye before doing so. He sat down with the old man.

Pavlo hadn't seen him since school, ten years or so ago. He couldn't tell whether Scababias had recognised him.

'What you want?' the baker asked Scababias.

'Nothing.'

The baker turned to Pavlo: 'Tough business, young man. How am I going to make ends meet? With these customers what you expect? Shitmunchers...'

Scababias stared at the baker.

'Don't you bloody look at me like that, Scababias. I'm not Betty. Got it?' Nevertheless, he backed off behind the counter.

Scababias withdrew his threatening glance from the baker and examined Pavlo, who was looking back at him.

'Bloody customers,' the baker said to Pavlo. 'And they give me a bad reputation.'

Pavlo turned around in his seat: 'Bad reputation?'

'Of course. Nobody wants to be around Betty and Scababias.'

'You scream at people and you threaten them that you'll break their fingers and you're a peado, and you're saying that it's because of these two that you get no customers?'

'Don't you fucking talk to me like that, young man...'

'I know you,' said Scababias.

The two young men locked eyes.

'Ah... He knows you...' the baker chipped in. 'I see, I see... Are you a shirt-lifter then?'

'I told you I like mums, nappy sniffer...'

'One more word and...'

'Give me the money. I want money. You promised,' Scababias said to the old man, cutting the baker short.

'I 'ave mo momey,' murmured the old man.

'QUIET!' screamed the baker.

'Child molester...' Pavlo called him.

'GET THE HELL OUT OF HERE! ALL OF YOU FUDGE PACKERS!'

Pavlo hurried outside the bakery, and yelled from the door: 'Kiddy fiddler!'

Scababias helped the old man out, and called him: 'Pavlo...'

Pavlo turned around. 'What?'

'Would you like to go somewhere for a drink?'

Pavlo pictured himself in a café with Scababias and Betty. 'No,' he said, and walked off into the storm.

The Beggar Who Travelled

1

Tolis was sitting on a park bench, half drunk, half sober, and half something else. He had enough supplies for the day's journey. His lame arm, the left one, was permanently bent in a sling-like lock, and he used the space between forearm and ribs as a shelf. He stored there, close to the heart as they say, bottles of *retsina* wine, takeaway frappes and cigarette packs of different brands, everything smeared with greasy fingerprints.

People were walking by. Tolis told them that Al Capone was cool, had a swig of wine, put the bottle back on the arm-shelf, and scratched his balls.

A passerby called out to him: 'What was Al Capone?'

'Al Capone was cool. *Cooooool!*'

'Ahahaha,' the passerby laughed. 'Ahahaha.'

'Look...' said Tolis, and stood up, struggling a bit to find his balance. He could only find his balance on his right foot, his left leg being lame, so lame that he couldn't put his shoe on properly and the big toe broke through the rotten laces and wiggled in the air. It was a sort of strange dance when he was trying to find his balance.

The passerby waited, smiling. 'Well, what is it?'

Tolis scratched his beard. 'Look. If you... Pardon me for asking, but if you ever go to a faraway place, can you bring me back a t-shirt?'

The passerby laughed and left, and Tolis sat down, his green eyes following the passerby, then gazing indifferently at the floor: a bird landed there, pecked at a crumb, flew away.

The sun moved lower, came out from behind a tree, hit him in the face—he moved to another bench. Not far, a motorbike with two lads slammed on its brakes, and the one in front shouted: 'Oi, Tolis! Do you like it up your arse?'

'I love it,' said Tolis.

'Hah, hah, hah! Did you hear? He loves it! Hah, hah!' the one in front laughed. Then the other at the back shouted: 'Tell us now, did they fuck you behind the bush? They fucked you, didn't they?'

'They turned my arsehole into a blooming carnation.'

The motorbike lads laughed and shot off, and Tolis drank, following them with his eyes. He lit a cigarette, puff-puff-puffed, saw a bird on the floor, staring up at him.

'Blooming,' he said to the bird.

'Hello, Tolis. You made them laugh,' said the bird.

'Hello, bird. Where is the one who understands?'

'He's near the sea. Find the sea.'

'Thaaaank you, little bird. Wait, don't fly away yet. I want to show you to him.'

'I'll peck around for a while. Tell me, what happened to your arm? To your leg?'

Tolis put his good hand into his shirt pocket and got out a pen and a little notepad, and steadied it against his thigh. He drew the bird on his notepad: 'It happened to me when I was little. Something struck me. Nice to meet you, little bird. Say chirp-chirp to your friends,' and the bird said that it would and flew away.

Now he wanted coffee and now he wanted alcohol and now he wanted smoke and now-now he wanted nothing and now-now-now he wanted everything and so he gulped down coffee and drank *retsina* and lit a cigarette, and he got up and danced and said to whoever happened to walk nearby that Al Capone was cool. He left his bench, limped down a few streets, glimpsed the blue of the sea, thought about the one who understands, made it to the harbour with the palm trees, sat on a bench and stared up at the palm tree. He stared at it for some time and people were walking up and down the harbour staring at Tolis, and Tolis went on staring at the palm tree for some time more. Having done that, he felt like staring at the palm tree for more-more time and so he lit a cigarette and stared at it from the depths of his soul.

'Hello, you,' the palm tree said.

'Hi...' Tolis smiled, and went on looking at it.

Tolis, Tolis, Tolis, will you be doing that for a long time, Tolis?

Yes, Tolis-Tolis went on doing that for a long-long time, especially as he had plenty of wine and coffee on his shelf. But then the palm tree said, 'Well, what do you want?' and Tolis was lost for words, and the palm tree said, 'Stop looking at me. Mind your own business.'

So, will you be doing that for much longer, Tolis?

No, because a group of barefoot Gypsy kids came up to him and called him names and threw unripe plums at him. Tolis hunched over his arm-shelf, and squealed: *'Aeeeeeee! Bad kids!'* The kids ran out of light ammunition and threw at him two rotten pomegranates: *plaf! plaf!* They missed the target.

The Gypsy kids pissed off.

Still hunched over, Tolis watched them from the corner of his eyes pissing off, walking under the first palm tree, the second, the third, the fourth and fifth, hardly seen under the sixth, tiny-tinier-tiniest, and as they walked on, the seventh palm began quivering... Startled, Tolis sat back: a beaky-beaky head popped up from the middle of its long leaves, and the palm tree craned its trunk, bent over the Gypsy kids and, one by one, it pecked at them with its beak and ate them. Once it had swallowed the last kid, it flapped its leaves against its trunk and took off for the blue of the sky. *Flap-flap*, it flew with its leaf-wings, *flap-flap-flap*, and looked down at Tolis: 'Tolis, Tolis, I ate them! Go now, you're near the one who hates his people but loves you, the way is free.' Tolis took his notepad out and quickly drew the flying palm tree bird. 'I'll give this to him, he'll understand that you helped me.'

He put the notepad back in his shirt pocket. He lit another cigarette and smoked it to the end and he liked it so much that he smoked another one. Lovely. Now: which one is his place, Tolis?

People were walking by, people people people, a woman with her whining boy kid. Tolis shoved his blackened nails into his beard and found the flesh of his chin and scratched it, eyes shut in pleasure: a woman with her kid. He stood up and danced his little dance of balance. A woman with her bad kid... hand in hand... coming towards him... 'BAD KID!' He limped towards the road, away from the harbour and the woman and the bad kid. One, two, three, four cars passed by, five cars. Blue, black, yellow, yellow, green. He let them pass by and stepped into the road.

'Aeeeeeee!' he squealed, crossing the road, 'The bad kid fucks his mum!' and away he limped, away away from the woman with the kid. He stopped, trembling, pulled out his notepad, and drew a kid fucking his mum, missionary position.

He ran-limped off, sensed that this was an unknown street, a street without benches. Away from the one who understands he ran. Away? No! He spun around, saw the bad kid. He spun around: yes, he had to, the boy kid was a genie who wanted to hurt him. He spun around: no, he wouldn't give in, he couldn't see any benches. Yes yes, he would, he didn't like genie-boys. No no, he wouldn't, he liked benches. Ah yes, he would. Oh no, he wouldn't. He spun around and around himself, until he felt sick. He raised his green eyes and saw how passersby had two heads, looking in both directions, and they had so many shopping bags that they needed four arms to carry them: they needed four, six, ten, twelve arms, they were standing up insects, and the cars drove through other cars, black through blue, and Tolis stumbled passed colours and insects, half petrified, half amazed, and half something else, crying and laughing at the stupid, scary town.

He vomited. He decided to walk through unknown parts of town, he advanced on hostile, benchless territories, carrying his beggarly stench with him, seeing things and things with his green eyes: his glassy-green and pickled-green and bombed-green eyes. Things and things he saw that made his something-else eyes wide-open in wonder, and squint in suspicion, and this in surprise, and that in boredom, and this in that, and that in this, and this and that and that and this, and—*bam!*—he crashed into a signpost… Oh…What's that, Tolis? That's a lovely, lovely bench, Tolis. By a taxi stand. Many, many orange taxis were queued there. He sat down, pulled out a cigarette, stuck it between his cracked lips, got the lighter, stroked the flint: *puff… puff puff.*

People again, people everywhere, people-people, a woman-people in a long, thin dress, a dress with flowers, a woman waiting, a dress waiting, not for a taxi, for something else, the woman and the dress waiting. The dress wasn't supposed to be that tight—*puff*. She must have put on weight and the flesh of her bum and breasts and thighs, all the nice, juicy bits, blasted about: she was sexy against her will—*puff puff*. While eyeing her, Tolis began fidgeting on the bench and felt some hairs around his arsehole cracking away from the rest of the arse-hairs that had been matted together with shit and sweat. He liked the sensation. He rubbed his bum on the bench to get more pleasure out of it. And as he eyed her breasts, something stretched beneath his balls, his cock grew longer, fatter, not hard yet, challenging him to go over and tell her: tell her and tell her. He made to stand up, when a bang shook his chest, and he felt his heart throbbing victoriously, a big, kind heart, beating all other senses into submission, making it clear who was the boss of that stinky carcass. So, instead, Tolis remained seated and whispered: 'I love you. I fuck you.' Longer his cock grew and his heart kept beating fast, working together now, heart and cock, heating up the wine in his arm-shelf, tainting the taste that burnt his tongue. Eyes shut, he swallowed the sweet pain, and stared at the woman: she stood, waiting, without the dress, the dress had been bored waiting, it probably went to meet with other dresses in shop windows. He took his notepad, drew her, shut his eyes, kept them shut. Opened them: so she hasn't moved yet... She's still waiting, Tolis... Take action, Tolis, while she's still here.

He crossed the good leg over the lame one and put his hand over his cock and rubbed it gently, and the woman stood waiting, and Tolis kept on rubbing, and when she saw him playing with himself, she looked him in the eyes, she looked him the way dogs looks at him, without judgment, and the dress came back flying and wrapped itself around her flesh and the woman and the dress walked away. She was a good woman, an angel woman of the dogs.

Away she walked, oh no!, but Tolis's eyes followed her, good little eyes… They narrowed and focused on her wobbling bum, oh my, when… when the fifth-in-the-row taxi-driver rolled down his window and shouted with his ugly voice: 'Al Capone get the hell out of here! You fucking pong, enough with you. Beat it! You listen to me? Beat it oh you better beat it right away!' and he rolled up his window.

It's one thing to be told off, but a completely different thing to be told off when you are horny. So Tolis became a bit stubborn and kept on smoking, *puff* he smoked, *puff! puff!* he smoked, blowing thick lines of smoke through his nostrils, *PUFF! PUFF! PUFF!* he smoked and the smoke burned as it rushed out from his nose's chimneys, and the green of his maddened eyes took over and he saw his hands green, his clothes, his shoes and skin, green, everything green, scaly-green, dragon-green, and *flap flap flap* he beat his right wing, the left one being sort of lame, *flap flap flap* now both his wings worked, and he flew, up into the sky he flew, the dragon-beggar, scanning the crowds for the angel woman of the dogs, searching for her, planning to steal her away from the one she loved, ha!, when… when the sixth-in-the-row taxi-driver rolled down his window and stuck out his slimy tongue: 'To hell with you! Oh you bloody skunk I've had enough oh to hell with you!' and he rolled up his window.

Tolis looked at the row of taxi-drivers and saw them all staring at him, violence in their small eyes.

Let's go away, Tolis. Why not? Yes, slowly-slowly… That's it, slowly-slowly…

He left. Kind-hearted buildings guided him back to familiar ground, he spread the word about Al Capone, making the townsfolk laugh, and some of them topped-up his shelf with new bottles and coffees and cigarettes and little snacks which he put in his pockets. The truth is that, while he was on the move, it was only some who told him to fuck off and fewer who told him that he took it up his arse. He drank and smoked and sat on many benches and walked many roads until he finally reached the terrace of Café Papaya, where he spotted a spoon on the floor. He picked it up with his long, bony fingers, and examined it against the setting sun: 'Hello, spoon. You are his.'

2

Pavlo had spotted the spoon on the floor, too, but he couldn't be bothered to stand up from his stool behind the bar. There were four or five customers outside on the terrace, pensioners, all served. It was a bit chilly now and they had draped their jackets over their shoulders. Pavlo scanned the customers to see how they reacted to Tolis's appearance. Not much reaction, they only fiddled with their noses. Good.

Without taking his eyes off the spoon, Tolis limped quickly inside the café.

'Hello, Tolis,' said Pavlo, and began breathing through his mouth. He had a handful of tricks to avoid Tolis's ruthless musty stench. Putting his nose out of action was discreet and usually worked for the short periods that Tolis's visits lasted.

'Look,' said Tolis. He offered the spoon to Pavlo. 'I didn't steal it. Stealing is not good.'

Pavlo thought that if anyone saw him taking a spoon from Tolis, Café Papaya would gain a very bad reputation. He took it.

Tolis screamed with joy. 'I brought the spoon to you. Look: the spoon is silver but the sun is orange.' He tangled his fingers in his brown, dirty, beautiful, his beautiful dirty-brown hair. He then rested his good elbow on the bar, chin on palm, and looked at Pavlo. He didn't do anything else, he just looked at him.

'Café frappé, takeaway?' Pavlo asked, and lit a cigarette to mask the smell. He gave three cigarettes to Tolis who put them inside one of the packs on his shelf and continued looking at Pavlo. Pavlo gave him another cigarette, and offered a light, and Tolis—*puff puff puff*—said:

'Yes, a coffee, please, my good child.' When he spoke like that, he didn't look crazy at all, his eyes were full of calm understanding.

Pavlo tried to look at Tolis with understanding, too, but he felt like an idiot, so he went back to looking at him in the normal way, and started making the frappé.

Tolis's eyes sparkled and turned crazy again: 'Look, Al Capone was cooooool. *Aeeeeeee!*'

Pavlo half-smiled. 'Would you like ice in your frappé?'

'Look. My brother is...'

'What is he?'

'Look. Maybe... Maybe you...'

Pavlo gave him a coin.

'My good child... Can you give me something to eat?'

'Yes, but on your next round. Now it's coffee time.'

'Look. This is for you.' He gave the full-of-drawings note-pad to Pavlo, who took his time looking at each drawing, trying to ignore the foul smell. He put the notepad it in his pocket, and handed him a new one. Tolis drew a naked woman with large breasts.

Pavlo said, 'I love your drawings.'

'What does it mean "I love"?' Tolis said.

'Right. Here's your frappé,' Pavlo ignored his question.

'Pardon me for asking, my good child, please, *paaardon* me, but "I love," what does it mean "I love"?'

'I don't know what "I love" means, Tolis.'

'What does it mean "I love"?'

Pavlo got on his knees, opened the cupboard in front of him, put his head into the dark, cool interior, took three deep breaths, got out, stood up: 'I don't know what it means.'

Tolis drew a naked woman and a massive cock going inside her, a cock so big that it touched her heart: 'This means "I love,"' and he danced, laughing a hysterical laughter mixed with screams.

While Tolis was screaming, Pavlo thought of sneaking another breath from the cupboard below, but he rejected this idea as in his panic he had forgotten to close the cupboard and the air inside had probably been infected. Instead, he breathed from the next cupboard, now having run out of cupboards. He stood up and said, 'You never sign your drawings. This is your best one. Can you sign it, Tolis?'

'What does it mean "sign it"?'

'It means write your name under your drawing.'

'I can't write,' said Tolis. He stood there, and didn't look like he was going to leave unless Pavlo showed him how to write his name.

Pavlo bent over the coffee powder and sniffed in, hard. With eyes bulging, he wrote Τόλης on a piece of paper, and showed it to him: 'Here. Now *draw* your name under your drawing.'

Tolis signed his drawing, tore off the sheet, put it in his mouth, and ate it.

Thunder was heard.

The beggar spun around and walked out of Café Papaya. Pavlo ran out onto the terrace to pick up the pillows from the chairs.

A great storm broke over the town of Kavala. A beautiful, September storm.

3

At midnight, Pavlo's shift finished, and he sat at the middle of the terrace for a last smoke. Angie, who had taken over for the night, brought him some ouzo. The storm had lasted for a long while, and the rain had come down hard, biblical. It had cleared the harbour of the townsfolk and the sea smelled more like sea. It was beautiful to sip ouzo under lemon trees and stars, taking your sweet little time on the peaceful terrace of Café Papaya, looking at the deserted harbour.

A war-cry was heard from faraway: '*Aeeeeeee!*' and soon Tolis's lanky figure appeared in the darkness of the harbour, waving at Pavlo with his good arm: 'Al Capone was cool!' He limped his way to the terrace. 'May I ask you something, my good child? Maybe… Would you mind if…'

Pavlo gave him a coin and his eyes fell on the beggar's left foot. It always bothered him a little that Tolis's big toe wiggled in the air, but now it got on his nerves. 'Stand still, Tolis.' He bent and took the beggar's sockless ankle in his hand, but Tolis began kicking and neighing.

'Did I hurt you, Tolis?'

'Look. My brother is...' he stopped.

Pavlo looked down at the wiggling toe. It looked like a happy toe, lonely but happy. He thought of his townsfolk and, staring at the toe, he said, 'Come over to my table, Tolis. Let's have some ouzo. Would you like that?'

And so, probably for the first time in his life, Tolis sat in a café, in the centre of the café, in its heart, with the man who understood.

Pavlo signalled Angie who brought ouzo for Tolis. While she was helping Tolis to remove the stuff from his arm-shelf, Tolis moved his eyes away from her breasts, and said, 'My brother is...'

'What is your brother?' asked Angie.

'My brother is...'

'That's where he stops, Angie,' said Pavlo. 'I've asked him a hundred times what his brother is and he never continues. Look,' he turned to Tolis: 'Tolis, what is your brother?'

'My brother is...'

'See?'

'Leave it to me,' said Angie. She took a seat, turned to Tolis: 'WHAT is your brother? WHAT is he?'

'My brother is bad.'

'WHY is he bad?'

'My brother hits me. He's a bad lad. He smashed my telly. He takes my coins and beats me up every night.' He turned to Pavlo: 'Look, can you buy me a telly?'

'I don't see why not.'

'Thank you, my good child. Thaaaaank you.' And to Angie: 'Look, if you ever go to a faraway place, can you bring me back a t-shirt?'

'What t-shirt?'

'You knooooow...'

'What? Like the ones that say *I Love New York*?'

'Yes, please, my good child,' he said, and sneaked a glance at her cleavage.

*

The beggar didn't smell that bad in the open air, it was bearable, and a fresh, soft breeze was coming from somewhere. No customers came and Angie brought some ouzo for herself and a large meze-platter for everyone. Tolis grabbed the pincers, picked up a big ice-cube, raised it high and let it drop into his glass, splashing ouzo all over the meze: 'My mother was kind. She loved me.' He gulped down as much ouzo as was left in his glass, filled it up, picked at a slice of ham and some fried onion: 'My children, you should love your mother.' He ate a salty anchovy fillet and his eyes turned crazy again: 'Al Capone was the best *gaaaaa-ngster.*'

With his fork, Pavlo pulled some chopped lettuce over the four pieces of red-wined octopus, burying them underneath the greenery. Angie replied to the men's advances on the meze by picking at cubes of feta cheese, to which Tolis responded immediately by going nuclear on the vine-leaf *dolma.*

'Al Capone was cool, but, you see...' Pavlo munched cabbage pickles.

'But, but? But what?' Tolis munch-munched.

Pavlo swallowed and half-smiled: 'But he *killed* people.'

'*Kiiiiill!*' Tolis rocked on his seat, stood up, danced, sat down, scooped at a variety of pickles, dropped them into the aubergine-cream, ate the whole lot.

'How about Al Pacino?' Angie asked. She went for the feta cheese again. She was keen on feta cheese. She must have had strong bones.

'Erm, look... Al Pacino was cool,' said Tolis. He ate a calamari ring, some fried onion, more ham, and half the potato salad: 'Al Pacino snorted coke. He had a big gun.'

Angie and Pavlo sipped their ouzo, Tolis downed it in gulps and he liked to fill his ouzo-glass to the brim, more than to the brim rather, he liked his glass to overflow. And when he got hold of it, you could tell from the way he held his glass that he was feeling something between glad and sorry.

'My mother... I loved my mother. She used to make me... Erm... She used to make me that food.' A wedge of Dutch cheese disappeared into his mouth. He picked at a black olive and swallowed it with the stone. Then he swallowed two more.

'What food?' Angie asked.

'My...' (he pecked at sundried tomato and feta cheese) 'favourite...' (devoured three slices of fried courgette) 'food!' (gulped down the smoked mackerel.)

Angie withdrew her fork towards taramosalata, scooped some: 'That was nice of her. But WHAT was it?'

Tolis swallowed two more olives, the way he liked it, with the stone.

'Listen, Tolis,' said Pavlo, 'these aren't Maltesers.' He sat back, examined the four pieces of octopus under the lettuce. They had been safe so far. He unearthed one octopus piece, ate it, had some tzatziki, sipped ouzo; repeated his ritual. The two remaining pieces were well-hidden under the greenery. He sat back, pleased.

'Now I want to know,' said Angie. 'What food was it, Tolis?'

'My favourite food...'

Angie ate a slice of salami with feta cheese, and screamed: 'WHAT food was it? WHAT?'

'It was food. Fooooood.' He picked at a hard-boiled egg. As he brought it with force towards his mouth, the egg came loose, flew in the air, hit him in the eye and, unbelievably, bounced back and fell inside his ouzo glass. He downed the ouzo with the egg. Then he picked at some bacon, over-filled his glass with ouzo, tossed in an ice-cube.

'Why does no-one eat the cucumber?' asked Pavlo. 'It's so healthy.'

Angie filled her mouth with chilli cheese-cream: 'But *what* food, Tolis?'

'Come on, Tolis, give us a clue.'

'It was like that,' said Tolis.

You'd expect him to make some sort of gesture describing the food, but Tolis just looked at Angie and said again: 'It was like that.'

'All right...' said Angie. 'What were its ingredients?'

'It was round,' said Tolis.

She lit a cigarette and looked at Tolis through the smoke: 'Meatballs? Was it meatballs?'

Tolis stopped eating and stared at Angie.

'What?' Angie asked.

Tolis stared at her.

'Was it meatballs then? Did I guess it?'

'It was green.'

Pavlo chipped in: 'Perhaps it was peas?'

'Green...' Angie murmured.

Tolis forked a stuffed potato and put it in his shirt pocket, with the fork. 'And red.'

Pavlo brought over another fork.

'My child,' he said to Pavlo, 'why do you hate your own people?'

'I don't hate them all, Tolis. I just feel very uncomfortable in their presence. Don't you?'

'Green and red...' murmured Angie. 'And what was it made of?'

'Inside it had... it had... Its *ingreeeeedients* were... Erm...'

Angie jumped: 'Yes, yes? What where its *ingreeeeedients*?'

Tolis said that Al Capone was cool.

'Hang on,' said Angie. 'Was is pep-'

'*Aeeeeeeee! Aeeeeeeee!*'

'Was it peppers, Tolis?'

'Peeeeeeppers!' He limped around the table screaming 'peppers' and sat back down.

'Stuffed peppers and tomatoes with rice? *Yemista*?'

'Yes!'

'We serve *yemista* here,' said Angie. 'Shall I get you some later to take away?'

Tolis stared at her. His eyes became misty.

'What is it?'

Tolis's eyes became mistier.

'Tolis?'

Pavlo put two cigarettes into his mouth, lit them, and offered one to Tolis. 'Don't you see, Angie? It's not *yemista* he wants. It's *his mother's yemista* he wants. You've upset him now...'

Angie insisted: 'Do you want some *yemista* for later?'

'Yes, please, my good girl,' he forked an octopus piece and nodded to Angie to pick the remaining one. With their mouths full, they smiled at each other.

*

And so they drank and talked and nibbled under stars and lemon trees and that fresh soft breeze still kept coming from somewhere, from a faraway magic place that creates soft breezes, when someone unexpected appeared: a taxi-driver, who walked through the terrace and shouted to Pavlo: 'Why do you let him sit in the café? He stinks! He's got a blotch of shit on the back of his trousers. He goes from bench to bench and leaves a stamp of his shit on the seats and no-one uses the benches after him. How do you expect people to come to the café when *he* is here?'

'There are people whose arses stink of shit and there are people whose mouths stink of shit.'

'What did you just say?'

But Pavlo had already said what he had to say, and the taxi-driver got the message and buggered off, shouting: 'You're as disgusting as him.'

Tolis got his notepad out and scratched his head.

'Do you think he'll draw the taxi-driver, Pavlo?' Angie asked.

Tolis scratched his chin.

'That's what I think,' said Pavlo.

Tolis drew a man walking, hand in pockets, who seemed to be whistling.

Pavlo asked, 'Who's this man?'

'Al Capone,' Tolis said.

'Can you do me a favour, Tolis?' Angie asked. 'Can you draw the sea? The Aegean Sea? I'm curious to see what you will come up with.'

'He doesn't draw like that,' said Pavlo. 'He needs inspiration.'

'Please, Tolis. Draw the Aegean Sea.'

Tolis drew a naked woman with long, wavy hair that reached down past her bottom. Her face was in profile, her eyes were squinting, as if she was trying to see something in the far distance, as if she was expecting someone, and she had four legs, one pair was closed, the other open. Then he drew St. Nikólas, watching her from behind. He scooped taramosalata and put it in his mouth.

'Tell me, Tolis,' Angie said, 'do you like the sea?'

Tolis shoved a piece of bread into his mouth and, whilst chewing, he said, 'I like taramosalata. *Aeeeeee!*' he squealed, '*Aeeeeee!*'

'What is it this time, Tolis?'

Tolis resumed drinking.

False alarm.

*

And now, the three of them, sitting under the trees of Café Papaya and the night sky of the Aegean, were bored of talking. So they didn't talk. They listened:

'*Chirp chirp chirp,*' chirped a little night-bird from a lemon tree.

'*Chirp. Chirp-chirp?*' another little bird chirped.

'*Chiiiiirp!*' a third little bird chirped in.

Having listened to this delightful conversation, they decided to finish off their ouzo and call it a day. And so they did: Pavlo downed it; Angie downed it; Tolis downed it—and said:

'I understand,' Tolis said, 'what does it mean, I understand?'

Pavlo and Angie smiled at each other. They wondered how to explain to him what 'I understand' means. They both thought of answering the way a dictionary would answer: I realise, I comprehend. They turned to Tolis, ready to give their answer, when Tolis said:

'I understand means I travel.'

The Round Table

I t was a sweet summer night with a cool sea-breeze blowing around the harbour. Without appointment, one after the other, some friends got together at the terrace of Café Papaya, around a big round table. They were four Egyptian fishermen and Pavlo, who stayed on after his shift finished. They talked about everyday stuff, drank beer. And as it happens sometimes on beautiful nights like this one, they began telling stories about women, just for the pleasure of it.

Their stories were short at first, half-forgotten images of this and that memory, stories defeated the moment they left their chests. As time passed by, though, each man began tasting that great feeling, the sense of having around you friends who wanted nothing more than to get on with you, and as they drank on and got well into the night, their stories grew bolder, ripe. They drank their beer, lit up their cigarettes, and one of the men drew a breath: 'Listen,' he said.

Up-Yours tells the story of a door
and what he found behind it

I go to this pussy-bar, the one further down the street from the police station. It's me and a friend of mine. There are two women at the bar. And the boss. One takes my friend to the booth. She's big, but my friend doesn't mind. The other woman comes to take me to the other booth, but she is very, very big. She's... I don't know how to say it in Greek, she's huge, she's big like a door. How's a door? *Wallah* she looks like a door. She tells me, 'Oh you sweet little thing, come with me...'

I'm scared of her and I want to leave. I say, 'One moment, please,' and I go to tell my friend that I want to get away from the door, but the woman that's with my friend whispers into my ear: 'Take her. She's good at sex.'

'Who's good at sex?' I whisper back. '*Mashallah*... She is?'

'Well, take her anyway,' she says. 'It's a sin to say no to a woman.'

The door comes in and takes me to the other booth. I'm shy to tell her that I don't want her. But I want to get away from her, so I tell her, 'Please, excuse me for a moment, I need the loo.'

'Come,' she says, 'I'll show you where the loo is.'

But I want to sneak out, I don't want to use the loo. Really, I want to escape from her. What can I do? I go to the loo and she follows me. I lock the door. The window in the toilet is too small—I can't escape from there. So I just stand, doing nothing. Anyway. Once I open the door, I bump into the boss: 'Can you help me?'

'No way. I'm straight.'

'Are you an idiot or are you mad?'

'Please stay away from me, I'm straight.'

'Straight? Why did you hire her? She's not a woman. She's... I don't know what she is, but she's like a door. I don't want her, but I'm too shy to tell her.'

'She was thinner when I hired her.'

'I want to leave and she keeps following me.'

'No problem, my friend. Look. Do you want this one?'

I look to the corner of the bar and I see this other girl. She must have been sitting behind the door, that's why I hadn't seen her. She's thin and wears a short skirt. 'All right,' I say. 'I want her. She looks nice.'

I go with the thin one to the booth and we have a drink and, as soon as we finish it, she says, 'Are you going to buy more drinks or shall I go?'

I say, 'Right. Let's have another drink.'

'But I won't have sex,' she says. 'I don't do such things. Let's clear up things first and then you buy me a drink.'

'And you think you can control me? Bring us more drinks and I won't do anything with you. I don't care about the money. When we finish the drinks, I'll just leave.'

She brings the drinks, sits close to me and begins talking to me. But I don't feel like talking, I say nothing. There's a song on the stereo and a story comes into my mind and I become very sad and I sing along with the song.

'You are in love with a girl,' she says.

'*Was* in love.'

'Why was?'

'Because before I come here, I broke up with her. That's why I came here.'

And that was true. She was my fiancée in Egypt. We had broken up over the phone and I smashed by mobile into pieces so that I couldn't call her again.

'Why did you break up?' she asks.

'Cool down,' I tell her. 'What's done is done, it's finished. Yesterday is yesterday. Don't you ask me again about it or I'll lose it.' And I feel like my mind shuts down and I become silent, I say nothing.

'Tell me,' she says, 'tell me about her.'

'Drink up your drink,' I say. 'After that, if you want to stay, stay; or if you want to go, go. No problem with me.'

And, lads, you know what she says then? Make a guess… All right, I'll tell you. She says, 'I want a hug.' Yes, that's right, she says, 'I want a hug.'

'You want a hug? Five minutes ago you said, "I don't do such things." So what you want now?'

'Just a hug.'

'No. I'm not in the mood.'

'Kiss me,' she says.

'No. Not allowed. Before you said that I'm not allowed to touch you, so now you're not allowed to hug me and not allowed to kiss me.'

She stays silent and stares at me. She just stares at me. Then she comes closer and puts her thigh over my cock and rubs it.

'What do you want?'

'A hug.'

To tell you the truth, at that point I've got a hard-on. I don't know what's going on: suddenly, she's in my arms, touching me here and there, caressing my hair, kissing me. Then she unzips me and takes my cock out. But I can't last long. I'm tired, for a whole month I hadn't done anything, for more than a month.

So I come quickly. But she keeps kissing me. And you know what? She takes her tits out and she takes her pants off and plays with herself. And she comes on her own.

You see, half an hour ago, I'm not allowed to touch her and now, now you fucking slut, now you come on your own?

Well, that was it, 'Goodbye,' I left the bar.

But afterwards I was sad. I didn't want to see anyone, I was gloomy and kept walking the streets in the night. No, not because I had broken up with my fiancée. Because I remembered the other one, the door. But I couldn't do anything with her. Honestly, I couldn't.

Pavlo tells the story where he and his friend come across a couple of prostitutes

I'm with the White Mohammed. We smoke hashish, then come here, to Café Papaya, about four in the morning. I'm not on duty. We drink *retsina*. And two women come and sit a few tables away from us. Are they having soup or drinks? What the hell're they having? One has got short hair, she's a bit plump and looks butch. She rides a bike as well. The other one is very pretty, fit and dark-skinned. They're whores.

And the White says, 'I can go,' he says, 'and break them women's balls.'

'Go on, then,' I say.

'No. You should go, you seem to know them.'

I kind of knew them, we'd say hi from time to time, because I'd serve them now and again when I was working the night shifts, but I didn't know them so well.

Well, another glass of *retsina* and then another one and then another and another... The White can take his booze. I can't. After the third or fourth bottle I'm bladdered. Stoned and bladdered. The White keeps teasing me, he says, 'Go, go, go. Tell them, ask them if they want to get fucked. You can talk well, you're Greek. And you know them, I can tell. They greeted you, they talked to you. Go on. Tell them.'

I still wonder how I found the courage to go over to their table. I sit down with them: 'Hello, hello,' I say. 'Could I possibly buy you a drink, ladies?'

And Butch says: 'Go straight to the marrow of the matter. Why did you come over? Usually you just give us a nod and that's it for the night.'

And I, what an idiot, I say, 'Why did I come over? What could you offer me?'

'Anything you like,' says Butch. 'Blowjobs, handjobs, front door, back door, anything you like.'

'Oh how nice... And how much would you like for these things?' I ask, 'Because it's me and my mate over there.'

'Thirty Euros each,' she says, 'is the basic fee. Now it depends on what you'll ask for.'

I return to the White and let him know what they're offering.

'Good,' he says, 'very good... So which one's mine, then?'

'I want the fit one,' I say. 'We could fuck her together, I don't mind. But with Butch I won't do anything.'

'No,' he says. 'I want the fit one.'

'Well, if that's the case, we'll sort something out, we'll make a swap maybe, we'll sort it out.'

I go to their table again. 'All right. Where would you like to go and do these things?'

'Let's go to a hotel,' Butch says.

'Let's go.'

We go to the hotel, enter the room. The fit one sits on a chair and Butch undresses and goes to bed: 'Right. Who's fucking first?'

'But we want to fuck your friend.'

'NO-ONE'S FUCKING MY BITCH!'

Man, she scared me. I turn to the White. 'Well, you go first then, White,' I say.

'Come on fuck me and piss off,' says Butch.

The White comes to me. 'No, no... You go first, Pavlo.'

'Please be gentle with her,' says the fit one from her chair.

'I think you should tell her to be gentle with us,' I tell her.

'I CAN TAKE IT,' screams Butch.

'Don't listen to her,' says the fit one. 'She's six-months pregnant with our baby. Did you take your baby pill, my love?'

Fucking hell. We left.

THEY ORDER ANOTHER ROUND OF BEERS AND THE BLOND EGYPTIAN TELLS THE LOVE STORY OF AN IDIOT AND A PROSTITUTE

Do you know this tall and skinny Egyptian with the bushy hair? He's my housemate. He's a very good lad, that's for sure. But, you know, he's naïve, he doesn't understand much, he's an idiot. This story happened a few months ago.

This guy had a relationship with a Bulgarian woman, you might know her, a very ugly one, short and fat, with a big, hooked nose... Ah, you all know her... So *you* know she's a whore, *I* know she's a whore, *everyone* knows she's a whore. But the idiot thought she was with him because she loved him. She kept telling him sweet words, you know, 'My love, my darling,' this kind of stuff, 'sweetheart, honey.' And he believed her. He believed that she loved him. And we all knew she was a whore, but whatever we said to him, the idiot wouldn't listen.

He kept giving her money, saying, 'I love you. Here, take this money, because I love you.' And this fucking bitch is even married, her husband and kids are in Bulgaria.

After a while, the idiot started to bring her home every night. I began hating her slowly, more and more by the day. I hated her for all the money and everything else that she took from my friend. I felt like beating her up. 'This is such a nice telly,' she'd say. 'You like it? Take it,' the idiot would say. 'Ah, this little table is so cute, honey.' 'I don't like it much, take it.' 'How about the stereo?' 'Take it.' 'Are you sure now?' 'Yes, take it.' 'And the salami in the fridge?' 'Take it. Take the whole fridge.' 'But how can I carry that?' 'I'll carry it for you.' 'Oh, you're so sweet...'

I returned home one morning and the sofa was missing. There was nothing left in the house. I sat on the floor waiting for the whore and the idiot to wake up. As soon as I saw the bitch I told her to get the hell out of my house. She didn't. She said, 'No, my love wants me here.' I called her names, very bad names, all the bad names that I knew in Greek. She didn't care. She said, 'I'll stay here. He loves me, I'll stay here.' I screamed that I didn't want to see her again at my house or around the harbour.

The idiot took the side of the whore. He looked at me with his big stupid eyes and told me that she wasn't a whore, that she was his girlfriend and that he loved her and that she loved him and that the house belonged to him too and that he wanted her to stay. He was telling me all that slowly, you know, as if *I* was the idiot. That made me angry. I shouted at him that his whore was dirty and stank. He replied calmly, 'No, she is not. She loves me.' I screamed at her to leave the house right away. 'No,' she said. 'He loves me. I'll stay.' So I began to kick her out.

But the idiot shielded the whore with his body. And then something bad happened. I can't remember exactly how it happened, because I had lost it completely, and when he told me, you know, very slowly, 'She…is…my…girlfriend… She…is…not…a whore… I…love…her… She…loves…me…' I grabbed him by the hair and banged his head against the window and the window smashed, and I can't remember how or why, I grabbed a piece of broken glass and shoved it into his belly.

And that's about it.

What happened after that?

I took him to the hospital. He told the doctors that he cut

himself by mistake. I don't think they believed him. They stitched him up and let him go. When he came back home, I told him that, for as long as he can't go to work, I'm going to give him whatever money I make at the caïque, I'll give him everything. I'm still paying.

And the Bulgarian whore? What happened to her, eh? Have any of you seen her around the harbour lately?

Pavlo remembers Rasool

I know this Bulgarian woman. Your housemate is not the only Egyptian who was after her. Listen, I know you Egyptians, I've worked here since I was fourteen. Do you know how many of you Egyptians I have seen over the years that at some point were after her, following her like mad? And do you know why? You're mad about the difference, about the contrast, about the mismatch, the uncommon, the unfamiliar. This woman has very pale skin and this is what makes many of you mad about not only her, but any woman with pale skin. Opposites attract.

Anyway. Now that I'm in the mood for preaching, do you want me to tell you about Rasool? Do you want me to tell you how whores can bring men from totally different places in a society onto the same level? And how they can bring a man to the lowest point?

I never liked Rasool. He was a terrifying-looking fellow, his eyes always scared me. I never felt like trusting him. I always put a barrier between us. But there was something I liked in him: that he was trying to find a different way of life from all of you Egyptians.

First, he went to work in the small boats that none of you had ever tried. There, he was getting paid better. Then, he left the sea altogether and got a job at a petrol station. It didn't work. Then he got involved with the undercover cops and tried to sell drugs. That didn't work either. We all know what happened to him.

Do you know why Rasool did all these things? Not only because he wanted to get away from the caïques or make easy money or I don't know what. He wanted to show off to Yuliya. He was madly in love with Yuliya, obsessed. He wanted to marry her.

Who was Yuliya? Yuliya was a typical Russian whore who had a husband and kids in Russia. As long as Rasool had money, she stayed with him. Once, I attempted to tell Rasool, to warn him, because it was obvious, plain as day that she was with him only for his money. But he got mad at me.

Then, one day, he came to me and said, 'Yuliya, Yuliya!'

'What happened?' I said.

'She stole my stereo, she stole my mobile and wallet and left. Tell me what to do. Shall I go to the police? What shall I do?'

He didn't go to the police. He couldn't. He wanted her back.

Then he tried to sell drugs and make big money and go to find Yuliya, but all he managed to do was get arrested and get deported back to the Egypt that he always hated. And that's another thing I liked in him: he hated his country. I hate mine. Anyway, he got deported and that was how the story with Yuliya ended.

But how did it begin? I know how it began, because I was working evening shifts when he and Yuliya kept coming here to Café Papaya.

It all lasted two months. I can't remember in which pussy-bar Yuliya was working, but at that same shithole, her close girlfriend was working too, some Ukrainian bitch. This friend of hers was shagging a guy who came here from Athens for a few months to refurbish the cinema. This guy, was he a civil engineer? A contractor? Whatever the hell he was, he was very well-off.

And look what happened. He came from Athens to Kavala, he went to a pussy-bar, met Yuliya's friend, and then the contractor, Rasool and the two whores were all together, one clique. For a couple of months you'd see them coming here to enjoy themselves: 'Bring ouzo, bring whisky, bring meze, bring bring bring. What do the girls want? Bring anything the girls want...'

Look now: on one hand you have Rasool, an Egyptian fisherman who by only looking at him you can tell he's a waster. And on the other hand you have the contractor from Athens with his expensive suits and nice car.

Both men paid the bills. But the one from Athens, you know, when he undertakes contracts to refurbish a cinema, he gets paid thousands. Rasool, an Egyptian fisherman who was working illegally here, how much money could he possibly earn, and how long would this money last him for?

Rasool was running out of money, but he was wearing himself out, too. He would work at sea for ten or twelve hours, come back, sleep for two or three hours, get up, have a cup of coffee, and then go off to entertain Yuliya. The contractor, what a cushy life—one hour he'd go to work, he'd say, 'This and that is what you need to do, guys,' and leave.

What a pair, eh? Contractor, Greek, successful, with the last scumbag of the harbour, well maybe not the last, but a scumbag anyway. So you see? Whores bring people onto the same level.

Rasool kept introducing his new friend to everyone: 'Oh, this is my friend, the contractor!' He felt so uplifted... He was living in a fairytale, but he took it for reality. He thought that Yuliya would stop working in brothels and that she would marry him and they'd be happy and have children together. And for friends they would have successful contractors.

Ah, Rasool, Rasool...

STRANGE SHIRT TELLS HIS STORY
WITH A BEAUTIFUL GREEK WIFE

I had this woman, she was Greek and married and very pretty. We had first met at a café and I'd bought her a drink and that's how our relationship began.

She told me she had never cheated on her husband. She said that her husband was the only man she had ever slept with. I believed her and I still believe her. 'What if he finds out that you see me now?' I asked her. She said that he probably wouldn't care. She said that he had stopped fucking her years ago. And I thought, how can a man stop fucking this beautiful woman?

In the beginning we were in love and I kept fucking her non-stop. I fucked her at her place, I fucked her at my place, I fucked her in her car, up the woods, down the Old Town by the rocks, at the Port Authorities, and I even brought her in the caïque and fucked her there. Then I got bored and got rid of her.

She kept calling me, but I told her I'd had enough of her.

And then she told me that she would even pay me to fuck her. I fucked her a couple of times more and got rid of her again. But she still kept calling me. So I passed her to other lads. And this beautiful married woman used to come to the caïques and get fucked by five or six lads at the same time. She would even drink the... the thing, what's its name, Pavlo? The white stuff, the milk? That's it, the sperm.

I remember one night she was down in the bunk beds, fucking, and I was on the deck, smoking and drinking tea. And I couldn't help it, but I couldn't care less.

THE BLOND EGYPTIAN TELLS THE STORY
OF AN UNFORTUNATE INCIDENT

I had this Greek girlfriend. She was young, sixteen or seventeen, maybe fifteen, I don't know, with glasses and long brown hair. She had some problems and was living in a madhouse. Her mum and dad had died and she kept talking to me about them. On the weekends the doctors allowed her to leave the madhouse and we'd meet, talk about her mum and dad, and fuck. Sometimes she'd bring me some of her madpills. I loved them. I got high on them.

She was the easiest girl to turn on. All I had to do was pinch her nipples and she got really horny. The bad thing was that, when we weren't fucking, she'd talk to me about her mum and dad. She told me everything about them, how they used to beat her up, put poison in her food, all that. When I'd heard everything ten or fifteen times, I couldn't take it anymore, I stopped listening to her. Whenever she'd start talking about her mum and dad, I'd pinch her nipples. 'Oh...

you see my mum and dad belted me on Thursdays... Aaaaah, mmmmm, I'm so hot, let's fuck!' and she'd jump on me. It worked for some time, but then I'd had enough pinching her and told her I was breaking up with her. She said nothing.

Then one night, about four months later, she texted me and asked me to meet at a bar in the Old Town to talk. I thought she might want to fuck. I hadn't fucked for a while, and I agreed.

So, I was on my own, walking towards our meeting place and it was very dark. And, you know, Old Town is full of narrow streets with no streetlights and low houses. I was walking... Suddenly, I looked up and I saw her up on a roof, holding a big stone. 'Aeeeeeeee!' she screamed. That's all I remember.

When I woke up the next day, I didn't know where I was. I saw people around me: 'Where am I?' They told me that I was in the hospital, but I couldn't remember how I got there.

I haven't seen her since. Here, look. I've got two naked photos of hers in my wallet. Look, that's her. Be careful when you walk around Old Town at nights. 'Aeeeeeeee!' Fucking crazy bitch.

THE MEN ORDER BEER, TAKE A GOOD LOOK AT THE PHOTOS, THEN PAVLO TELLS A STORY ABOUT SELF-EXPRESSION

I'm in bed with this girl. It's our first time. She's Greek. We get naked, but I don't feel like fucking her.

'Why don't you fuck me?' she says.

'I don't know.'

'What you mean you don't know? Fuck me.'

'Maybe I'm not in the mood,' I say.

'Not in the mood? Here, grab my boobies,' she says. 'Here, here,' and she takes my hands and puts them on her boobs. 'Grab them. Harder. You like?'

They're nice, but I still don't feel like fucking her.

'Bite my nipples then.'

'All right,' I say, and bite them.

'Harder!'

I bite harder.

'AH YES YES HARDER!'

I stop biting. I was biting so hard I thought I might chop her nipples off. Anyway. I still don't feel like fucking her.

We stay in bed, we don't talk.

After a while she sits up and says, 'I want you to express yourself. Feel free, darling. Why don't you feel free? Just express yourself.'

'How do you want me to express myself?'

'How? Just express yourself,' she says again. 'Do you want to hit me? Hit me!'

I say, 'All right, I'll express myself.'

I get off the bed and I sit on a chair. I tell her to come over. She comes. I tell her to drop to her knees and give me a blow-job. She goes down, but she's not on her knees, she squats.

'Why don't you get on your knees, babe? I'd love to see you on your knees...'

'I'm fine just as I am,' she says abruptly.

Then she takes my cock in her mouth and works on it and I get hard.

'That's it. Suck it, slut. Oh yeah, you fucking whore...'

Once I say that, she takes my cock out of her mouth, gives

me a very serious look straight in my eyes, and says: 'I didn't like that.'

'But, babe,' I say, 'you know I didn't really mean it, don't you?' and I start explaining why I had I called her names like that.

By the time I finish explaining, I'm not horny any more. I doubt she was horny anyway.

We go back to the bed. We don't talk. But this idea about expressing myself is still buzzing in my head. I really feel like expressing myself. So, I tell her, 'Do you know what I want now?

'What? To hit me?'

'I want you to give me a handjob. An oily handjob.'

She says nothing.

I take her silence as a yes and take the baby oil and give it to her. She pours some on my cock and begins rubbing it. I begin getting hard: 'Oh you little slut...'

She works on it, but I'm not very happy. The way I like it is with plenty of oil. Lots of oil. I want everything to be very slippery. I take the bottle and try to pour more on my cock and balls and she grabs my hand, and screams, 'Enough! Enough oil! That's more than enough!'

'What's the problem now? I like it oily.'

'I DON'T WANT TO GIVE YOU A HANDJOB!'

'YOU'D BETTER GIVE ME A HANDJOB NOW!'

'No! No! No!' she says, and runs away.

I'm still horny: 'Oi, you bitch! Get right back here and give me a handjob!'

'Or what? You'll hit me?'

'Yes!'

'Hit me then!'

I slap her hard across the face. She spun around.

'Not that hard! Oh, you sick bastard!'

She left, and I expressed myself on my own.

UP-YOURS TELLS OF A SMALL INCIDENT
FROM HIS VILLAGE IN WHICH THERE ARE MORE SLAPS

While listening to this story, do you know what I was thinking? That it's nice to have a girlfriend and not to sleep with whores all the time. In Egypt I never had a girlfriend. None of us here had. Egypt isn't Greece. You aren't allowed to have girlfriends. So I've never had one. Not one. I've been engaged three times, but even when you're engaged you aren't allowed to fuck your fiancée. Not even kiss. Not even hold her hand. With whores I've been, yes. But to have a girlfriend in Egypt is impossible.

One day, back in our village, in Ezbit El Burg, I saw a pretty girl in the street and, once I saw her, I forgot everything, our customs, our religion, everything. I went and asked her if I could buy her a coffee.

'You're a donkey!' she said.

You see, Pavlo, this is how things work there—the lads know. It's like that: the girl swears at you at first, this is supposed to be cute and you're supposed to laugh, and finally you might ask your family to go and ask her family if you and your family are allowed to have a cup of coffee with her and her family.

But I was so tired of all that shit that when she called me donkey, I slapped her. Two old women saw that and came to tell me off, and I slapped them too. Then some men came and I spat in their faces and ran away.

The girl told her family and they called the police. Police went to my village, they were looking for me for days. But they couldn't find me. Nobody knew where I was. Even I didn't know where I was. I took my cousin's little rowing boat and rowed far out to sea. Four days and four nights I stayed at sea. Not because I was scared of the police, but because I was sad about everything.

Since then, I've never tried to get a girlfriend. I just sleep with whores.

One Arm tells his story from Alexandria

Not everywhere in Egypt is like that, Up-Yours. When I was nineteen, I lived in Alexandria for a few months, and there I had a girlfriend and we were living together and we were sleeping together and we did everything together. But this story isn't about me and my girlfriend, it's about another girl.

My girlfriend had a close girlfriend who would fuck every day with a different man. Or maybe the same man for some time, but she had to fuck every day. She was a fucking machine. She wouldn't stop. She wore hijab and niqab and everything, but she was fucking non-stop.

At some point, she got into a relationship with a lawyer from Cairo. She fucked so much with him that she had three abortions. She on was the pill, but her pussy was so powerful that the pill wouldn't work. Then I don't know what happened with this guy from Cairo and they broke up, and she fucked any man available. One night she went in a European bar to find a man to fuck, but she couldn't find any one, so she fucked with a woman.

Another night, me and my girlfriend we invited her to my place for dinner. We had dinner, then sat on the sofa to watch my girlfriend's favourite TV show. 'I didn't fuck today,' she said. 'OK, hold it for one day,' my girlfriend said. Halfway through the show, this girl said, 'I need to use the loo,' and went to the loo. The show finished and the girl still hadn't come back. We checked the toilet, she wasn't there. We went to bed to sleep, and this girl pops up from under the covers, all naked, smiling: 'Hello, guys...'

UP-YOURS TELLS A STORY ABOUT FORGETFULNESS

I've never been to Alexandria. I've only been to Cairo once with the school when I was seven to see the Pyramids. I don't know what's going on in Alexandria or in Cairo, but in our village you never do these things. When you're young you want to do everything, to kiss, touch, fuck, everything, but you don't dare. And when people grow up, when they get old, they forget what they wanted to do when they were young. They forget everything.

My older brother—I've got eight brothers, my older brother who's fifty now and he's married and has children—had worked here in Kavala for a few years and then made some money and went back home.

A thousand times he tells me on the phone, 'Come back. Don't stay in Greece anymore.'

He says that because I never send any money back to Egypt. I spend all my money on the whores.

Whenever he calls me, he says, 'You give them whores a lot of money.'

I say, 'I have to fuck. If I don't fuck, I'll wank.'

One night, I'm drunk and I bring a whore home, the Bulgarian with the nose… And I call my brother.

'How are you, my brother?' I say.

'I'm good,' he says. 'How are you? How's it going?' He then says, 'Why don't you send money here? Where is your money? Spent on whores?'

I say, 'So, my brother, when you were here, didn't you go to the whores?'

'Keep your voice down. My wife is here, she'll hear!'

'No problem,' I say, 'I won't say a word. Talk to her.' And I give the phone to the whore.

'How are you Mustafa, sweetie? All right?'

'Who's that?' my brother screams.

I take the phone, 'It's Mirela, the Bulgarian. She told me about you. Don't you remember Mirela, my brother?'

His wife was nearby and overheard.

'Who's that woman on the phone?' she asks, and they argue. Before he hangs up he says to me: 'Yiak! Don't you dare to come back to Egypt!'

AFTER SOME PROMPTING, STRANGE SHIRT TELLS THE STORY OF A TALKATIVE BOY

I'm about to drive from our village down to Cairo, when my mama brings this boy over. She says he's my cousin and he's very bright and he's going to Cairo to study in the university. I had to take him with me.

I drive off and this boy keeps on talking and talking. He gives me a headache. I ask him to stop it but he goes on talking for hours and I'm driving. I tell him I like it quiet in my car and he says all right and then goes on talking again. I ask him to please shut up and he says yeah right and talks again. Halfway to Cairo, I stop the car and drag him out. I make him bend over the hood and fuck him. We get back in the car and I drive off. He didn't say a word after that.

ONE ARM CLOSES THE CIRCLE OF SUMMER NIGHT STORIES WITH A STORY ABOUT HIS WIFE

There are a few guys here that are very strict Muslims. If they see someone doing something that they don't like, they tell people back in our village.

Once, I go back to Ezbit El Burg to see my family, and my wife says to me, 'You've been with women in Greece!'

'Me?' I say, 'No. Never.'

'Do you swear? Say *wallah*.'

'What's there to swear about? I've never been with women. Why do you say that?'

'That's what I've heard!'

'From whom?'

'Someone came to me,' she says. 'He knows you in Greece and he said that you are a big slob in Greece and every day you go with women and every day you drink beer and every day this and every day that.'

'My love,' I say, 'I sometimes drink a glass of whisky. So what? It doesn't really matter. Where's the harm in that? It's because I get tense and I need to relax, to calm down. Yes, I've had a glass of whisky, but with women, no, I've never been with women.'

'No! You've been with women!'

'All right. You believe what this guy said to you. You don't believe me. If you don't believe me, why do you ask me?'

She says, 'Do you swear that you didn't go with women?'

'Why swear?' I say.

She says, 'If you don't swear, it means that you've been with women!'

Well, I think, I'll tell a little lie. What else could I do? I did it so that she'd stop complaining: '*Wallah*, I didn't go with women.'

'All right,' she says. 'Now I believe you.'

*

It would dawn soon, and each man had to take his own way home and face the reality of the day, the misery of their single beds. Tired, they sat back around the round table, just to enjoy for a little longer this sweet summer night, remembering with pleasure the stories they've shared, sucking back the smoke of a last cigarette, feeling free.

The Story-Gatherer's Caïque Voyage

One Arm finished telling his story to Angie and they looked out to the sea. She washed his beer glass, put the bottle in the returns crate, and they left Café Papaya. They walked under the warm evening sun, over to the harbour and the caïque Cappa. The caïque's engines were on, with its crew lounging about the land beside it, and the fisherman with the sliced-off arm had a word with the big man with the sparkling earring, Captain Cappas. A little later, the captain whistled for the fishermen to board, Angie followed, and the voyage began.

The few locals who sat on the harbour's benches watched the caïque with the girl on its stern heading slowly for the open sea. She stood by the balustrades, keeping clear of the men who were carrying about wooden cases, rounding up mooring ropes. She turned back, to her town of Kavala, and her eyes searched for the one-armed fisherman: he waved at her and walked back to the café.

From the other side of the harbour, a small motorboat sped towards the caïque, and the man who piloted it began performing trick manoeuvres.

'CUT THE BULLSHIT,' Captain Cappas said through the megaphone.

When the motorboat got closer, Angie recognised one of her regulars from the café, a young Egyptian who had the usual withdrawn bearing of the fishermen when he drank his coffee, but when he told her stories, there was a spark in his voice, and something of a melody, easy on the ear. His name was Mohammed, but everyone around the harbour

195

called him Up-Your-Arses. He trailed the caïque with the motorboat and threw a rope onto the deck, and the fishermen tied it to the sternpost. He passed four or five plastic water barrels up to them, then clambered up onto the deck. Captain Cappas increased speed and they passed beyond the harbour's mouth and out into the Aegean Sea.

Angie remained by the stern, watching the fishermen and the sun-drenched Aegean. From time to time, the four Egyptians of the crew would leave their jobs and go over to have a word or two with her. She knew them from Café Papaya, the harbour-side café where all the Egyptian immigrants who worked on the caïques liked to spend their mornings, smoking and drinking the coffee Angie made for them, now and then telling her stories in their heavy accents: they were simple stories about the sea and the fish, told slowly, in a few, tired words, and even on the rare occasion they spoke of the Aegean's black squalls and night-fogs, their eyes remained passive. But in the evenings, those who stayed ashore liked to smoke hashish and go to the café to drink beer and ouzo, and their tales were confusing, dreamlike. Then Angie would see their eyes glisten strangely and she would listen, and listen again as they told her of their fishing village that stands where the Nile becomes the sea, a village with a thousand wooden caïques, marked with symbols and painted with large female eyes with long eyelashes or the eyes of eagles. With beer and hashish inside them, their ramblings rattled of the caïques of Ezbit El Burg, so many that even the great river that used to be a God wasn't wide enough for them. And as night fell on the harbour of Kavala, their money spent, their beer bottles empty on the table, the drunk ones had nothing but threads of memories to hang on to, and they would call out the name

of Allah and their hard faces would soften with sweet hope:
then the waitress knew that the time had come for them to
murmur their caïque-dreams and remember old sea-voyag-
es to Falasteen, and down and beyond the Red Sea, when
they first saw the shores of Sudan and Habasha, of Yaman,
of Djibouti and Alsomal. The young girl listened to their stories with large, impressionable eyes, she listened and learnt.
And it was in one of those waitressing nights that Angie had
asked if she could join them on a voyage, to live one of their
stories. Months passed, and she thought they had forgotten
about it with their drunkenness, but the Egyptians remembered and waited, knowing that Angie wouldn't enjoy it on
the long and hard winter voyages, they waited for the spring.
They remembered, because they respected Angie, for she was
fair with them, swift with the tray and good-mannered, and
she never used swear-words, although she grew up working
around the harbour and knew the harbour-life well.

*

These four Egyptians who worked on caïque *Cappa* were
all called Mohammed and the waitress had come up with her
own private names for each of them: the Mohammed with
the Moustache, the White Mohammed, the Strange Shirt; and
Up-Your-Arses was the fourth Mohammed. Then there were
her fellow locals who, with the exception of Captain Cappas,
hadn't uttered a word to her so far: a very old, skinny and en-
ergetic man who seemed to be in his eighties and whom the
Egyptian fishermen called the Mummy, and a middle-aged
one who had lots of teeth missing. These two had been in the
tiny galley all along, chatting and drinking iced coffee. The

fourth Greek was a lad, the mechanic, who didn't speak to anyone. He only sat by his winch, smoking and fiddling with the machinery, sometimes gazing around, but keeping his eyes away from everyone.

In the middle of the deck, out of the way, a chubby old man with an ashen beard was sitting on a very low wooden stool. Angie had never seen this one before and she couldn't tell from his appearance whether he was Egyptian or Greek. The thumb of his right hand was missing, and he was holding a dagger and a small piece of net, trying to bind the snapped arm back to his spectacles.

And there was another Egyptian in the crew that she hadn't seen since the caïque had departed, a giant of a man with wild hair that harbour-people called by a name neither Egyptian nor Greek, Zaramarouq.

And so, the wooden caïque with the ten men and the one girl changed course, and propelled its way past the dark green Island of Thassos, heading towards the setting sun, searching for fish.

*

They were far from the town, her eyes had adjusted to all that blue around her. The Egyptians signalled for her to join them, and they sat on the decking near the bow. They lit cigarettes and smoked, and talked about the everyday stuff. The Mummy and his friend left the galley and headed with new frappes towards the trapdoor. As they were passing by the Mohammeds, Up-Your-Arses said, 'Hi, Tutankhamun.'

'Hello, twat.'

'Why didn't you stay home to die together with your wife?'

'I'm making money to go to Egypt to fuck your mum.'

'She's dead.'

'I'll fuck her bones.'

'It'll hurt.'

'Fuck off, tosser,' said Tutankhamun, and dashed to Up-Your-Arses and pinched him in the belly and on the ribs, something that the middle-aged Greek found so funny that he showed his gums. The two Greeks went down to the bunk beds. The young mechanic oiled the winch, running a cloth slowly along its metal tubes, and his eyes met momentarily with Angie's, but Angie couldn't tell whether this brief meeting of glances expressed friendliness or hostility.

'Tell me,' she asked the Egyptians, nodding towards the old man with the ashen beard, 'who's this man? He's such a sweet grandpa.'

'Him new here. He can't speak Greek,' said the Moustache. 'He's from Falasteen. He don't know how to mend the nets. He's not a fisherman, he's—how you say it—the man is a sailor.' He said that the old Palestinian was one of the six sailors from a Russian ship flying a Lebanese flag and that his ship was impounded a week ago in the nearby port of Karavali.

'And how did he end up here?'

'I'll tell you later,' the Moustache said, and joined the rest of the Egyptians who had gone back to mending the nets.

Angie found a comfortable spot in between some cases, and watched the old Palestinian man who was doing nothing, just sitting on a very low wooden stool. Then she walked over and he stood up and offered his little stool to her. She declined, and the two of them sat on the decking, opposite each other.

The old sailor raised his big hands: 'Karavali,' he said— the name of the port where he had gone ashore.

'Calamari?' Angie misheard. 'I don't understand. Calamari?' She pointed at his hand with the missing thumb and made an eating gesture: 'Calamari did this?'

'Bah...'

The old Palestinian stood up, leaned on the gunwale. The image of the sea collapsed something inside him and he sighed, 'Ah, *Yarab, Yarab...*' He looked at the fading light of the ending day and said a few more words in the language of the Arabs. Then his gaze invited her to look far, and he smiled in a sort of confidence with the sea, as if somewhere out there in the blue, his Palestinian eyes were seeing something that Angie couldn't. She felt a little sad, for she couldn't see the beauty he could see.

Up-Your-Arses went over and opened a new pack of cigarettes: 'Have one, Angie.'

Captain Cappas' voice was heard, loud and distorted by the megaphone:

'FINISH OFF WITH THE BLOODY NETS AFTER YOUR SMOKE.'

'We need to take a break, boss,' Up-Your-Arses shouted back.

'YOU NEED A COCK UP YOUR ARSE, THAT'S WHAT YOU NEED. ARSEHOLE. I SAID, "AFTER YOUR SMOKE."'

They smoked, and the old sailor took Angie and they sat close to the Egyptians, watching how they worked their needles around the nets.

'Look, Angie,' said the White Mohammed. He cut a cord from the net and took his time plucking out hair from the Palestinian's eyebrows.

'Show me,' said Angie.

The White took Angie's hands into his and they worked

together on the fishermen's sideburns and eyebrows. The old Palestinian taught her nautical knots and the Strange Shirt how to sew up new nets. They stayed focused on loops and meshes, and when the dark began to settle around them, they were still leaning over the nets, feeling in their fingers the needle and the cord.

*

Above them the new sky raised its magic flag of yellow stars and a thin, silver moon, marking its territory with darkness and shadows. And the caïque glided on in the night, wood against waves.

Back on the stern, two Egyptians climbed up the iron structure that held a small lightboat. They pulled back the canvas and Zaramarouq the giant woke up. Captain Cappas switched off the engines and all the lights, the caïque free to flow with the sea current now.

The two Egyptians lowered the lightboat into the choppy sea. Zaramarouq washed his face with seawater and fitted the kerosene pressure light on the stern of his little boat, and lit the lamp. Soft white light broke the darkness. Soon, little fish appeared below the illuminated zone, milling around the light, opening and closing their little mouths. He steadied the oars in the iron hooks and slipped them softly into the water. More and more fish swam up from the depths, crazy for artificial light. Zaramarouq stood up and began with careful strokes, long and steady, and with each stroke of the oars the sea gave a sound of pleasure, and the fish followed, trapped in the light. A little while later he had rowed into the darkness.

The crew had three or four hours to kill until Zaramarouq finished luring the shoal of fish. The Strange Shirt went to the galley to prepare the dinner. The rest started their own private fishing.

Angie wandered about the deck. The Palestinian grandpa gave her a sweet smile, and she offered him cigarettes. The young Greek mechanic looked away.

She went to the tiny galley. The Strange Shirt was cooking in his yellow shirt, which had lots of tiny crocodiles on.

'Hey,' she said, 'that's a nice shirt.'

'You like?'

'It's strange. Can I give you a hand with the cooking?'

'No, no. You're a—what's the word—a friend, a visitor here. This is my job. I'll do the cooking. Please, you just re-lax.'

'Can I watch how you cook the rice? They say Egyptian style rice is really tasty.'

'Not here. Here not good. Too small here. Come to my place one time. I'll show you.' He winked at her and she laughed.

Angie joined Up-Your-Arses and the White. They had caught small fish, sea-breams mostly, and a few bogues. Up-Your-Arses gave the line to Angie and she took it in her hands. 'Ah, no, no. Not like that,' he said, and she felt the net-scars on his palms as he took her hands into his: 'Let me show you...'

He showed her, then Angie went to the bow. There, bal-ancing on the gunwale, stood the Moustache and Captain Cappas, holding their fishing lines, staring down at the wa-ter in silence. Half of the captain's bum crack was out on view. The Moustache began pulling up his line with long and swift moves, until a calamari sprang up from the sea. He un-hooked it and jumped back on the deck. He held it in his one hand and caressed it with the other, then offered it up to Angie: 'See how beautiful that feels.'

'Is it necessary?'

'You are no girl here. You are a woman of the sea.'

She took it in her hands, reluctantly. It must have been alive, but it was motionless and covered in slime. She looked at it, caressed it the way the Moustache did, searching her feelings, trying to find beauty in that helpless creature. Once again, she only felt a little sad; there was nothing there for her to find, beauty escaped her.

*

The waitress lay down on the deck with her hands behind her head and closed her eyes on the night, while from behind the galley came the strong smell of fried liver. The Strange Shirt came out of the kitchen: 'Food ready. Follow me.'

They hung a lamp on a pillar and sat on the decking, around a low and round wooden table. But, again, the Greeks didn't join them. The captain went up to his wheelhouse, while the young mechanic, Tutankhamun and his friend with the gums stayed down on the bunk beds.

The Strange Shirt brought out so many aluminium bowls, that they had to bunch them together to fit on the table. There were bowls with fried chicken liver with oregano, bowls of rice, fried eggs, tomato and cucumber salad, and a big one with sliced bread. Finally, the Strange Shirt brought a bowl with fried Frankfurter sausages and placed it by Angie: 'That's only for you,' he said.

They were eating and chatting and laughing, and the sea was calm and the night cool. The light from the hanging lamp reflected on the aluminium bowls and made them shine, so that the table gave out a silver glow. Angie stopped eating, and said, 'Look. The table has a soul.' The fishermen smiled. She looked at their faces, illuminated by the silver glow as they reached over to help themselves from the bowls, half-hidden in shadows as they sat back to chew. In the silver darkness their skin appeared metallic, the lines on their brows and around their eyes formed deep cracks, and she felt that something was waiting to be seen, to be discovered in those cracks, something like a secret. Her eyes searched the crust of their skin, trying to see through those cracks and catch the glimmer of another world, until, once again, she felt that sadness of the locked away beauty. The Egyptians nudged her: 'Eat, girl. Eat,' they all said. 'We're so glad you're here with us.'

The Strange Shirt pointed to the bowl with the sausages: 'Is this pork or the other meat—turkey?'

'I guess it's pork.'

The Strange Shirt turned his head away. 'The captain bought all these packets of sausages and told us they were turkey,' he said. 'Because we're Muslim and not allowed to eat pork. He can say anything he likes, we can't read Greek.'

Angie said that perhaps it was turkey, but the Strange Shirt motioned her to stop. 'It doesn't matter now,' the fisherman said and lit a cigarette.

They all leaned against heaps of nets and piles of wooden cases, and inhaled the tobacco in silence around the silver table, until, one by one, they threw the butts away and went down to the lower deck, to the bunk beds, to sleep.

*

But Angie didn't dare go down with the men and stayed on the deck on her own. They didn't insist, they understood. She looked at the shadows of the deck, at the round table, now propped in a corner. A *meltemi* wind raised, it whistled, and she felt as if the wind that blew cold in her face was trying to tell her something—and she didn't look for shelter. She stood by the balustrades, near a wooden pillar, as motionless as the pillar itself, trying to catch the meaning of the whistling wind, shivering, living the voyage story. She raised her eyes and looked at the vastness of the dark sea and realised she was out there, far from her town. She remembered the locals on the harbour who had seen her leaving with the fishermen, and she felt proud, then ashamed, then proud again. She looked up towards the stars, began counting them to try and forget the cold, got bored, her gaze fell back on the sea. Her eyes caught a tiny white light, far away, it was moving slowly across the darkness of the sea, and she stood, stubborn, with strands of her long black hair dancing like seasnakes in the wind, her gaze nailed on the white light, her eyes the eyes of the caïque, big, dark, honest eyes: *Be careful, Zaramarouq.*

And the silence of the deck was broken by a slow creaking sound. She turned back and saw the caïque opening up its heart, and from beneath the trapdoor's musty darkness, two Egyptians climbed up the steps.

'We came to keep you company.'

They were the White Mohammed and Up-Your-Arses, bringing blankets, cans of drinks, bags of sunflower seeds, a pocket radio. They spread out a blanket and Angie sat on

it. They placed another blanket over her shoulders and sat by
her side.

They all stayed silent, only breathing, the sea in their dark
eyes.

The White Mohammed poured salty seeds onto their
palms. Up-Your-Arses tuned the radio into a station that
played old Greek love songs with dedicated messages.

Angie laughed.

'Why do you laugh, Angie?'

'Why do they call you Up-Your-Arses?'

'Or, Up-Yours, for short. One day I did some bullshit and
the police arrested me and put me in the prison. I liked it
there, we could watch telly sometimes, and they brought us
nice food and iced coffee. But after a week or so they decided
to let me go, and gave me a paper to sign. I can't read Greek,
so I wrote in Arabic, *fi teezakoom*, which means *up your arses*.
As I was leaving, I told them, "Go and find out what my sig-
nature means." I wanted them to put me in jail again. They
found out about it and got angry. But, by then, I had changed
my mind about having vacations in the prison. I went into
hiding. They began looking for me at the harbour, describing
me, asking about the Egyptian who wrote in Arabic up your
arses. That's how the name stuck with me. I'm Up-Your-Arses.'

There was a heap of nets behind them, and they rested on
it. Up-Yours sang along with the love song on the radio with
his Egyptian accent, half-mocking the singer's emotive voice
and half-feeling it, making the others laugh.

The White motioned to him to switch the radio off. He
leaned in: 'Listen...' he whispered as if he was going to tell
sea-secrets. 'Do you feel the silence? When I go on a voyage, I
don't think of my family back in Egypt or my girlfriend back

in town, I feel like I'm going home. When I'm here, I feel safe, sea is my home and the silence of the night sea belongs to me.'

'When I'm here,' said Up-Yours, 'I'm not Egyptian, I'm not Muslim, I am myself and nothing more. To hell with everything.' He looked up at the sky and shouted at the stars: 'Dedicate a song to us! To Angie and the two Mohammeds, who are free in the middle of the sea!'

They lay down on the deck and covered their bodies with the heavy blanket, Angie in between the two fishermen, and, like that, they fell asleep.

*

Before Angie had fully woken up, the picture on the deck had changed completely. The engines were running and strong yellow light hit her eyes. Down on the horizon, the brightness of the dawn was claiming the sky back, and the *meltemi* wind had grown stronger, spraying seawater into her face.

'Go down to the bunk beds, Angie,' the Moustache said.

'I want to stay here.'

'Then stay out of the way.'

Everyone was on the deck. They had changed into waterproof uniforms, rubber boots and thick gloves, and had positioned three large white containers in the middle of the deck. Dozens of piles of wooden cases stood close by. The winch moved and groaned, the young Greek sitting on his high chair, throwing Angie daring glances.

'THERE'S PLENTY OF FISH DOWN THERE,' the captain said.

The fishermen carried the long net towards the bow and supported its edge on the hauling drum that hung above the sea. Everything was ready for the first catch, the first *kaláda*. The sea grew stormier and swelled, as if it didn't want to have its fish taken away, and its waves raised and curled, and lashed down on the caïque.

'*NOW LET IT ROLL*,' ordered the captain.

The mechanic pulled a lever and the net plunged into the sea, and the caïque lurched forwards, while the crew spread out along the starboard side.

'Now!' shouted the mechanic.

The caïque changed course, circling. A big wave crashed against the hull and the caïque jerked as spectacular splashes of water hurled towards the sky. Foam was running along the deck, making it slippery, and Angie felt her stomach stiffening and she doubled-up. Through the noise and the clatter and the dazzling of the yellow lights, a voice reached her ears: 'Angie, find the horizon and look at it. Just look at it and you'll feel better.'

The crew bent over the balustrades and began dragging the net, their upper bodies hanging above waves that hissed, Mohammeds, Tutankhamun, the man with the gums, the old Palestinian sailor, the net, the sea, their arms for the fish: they dragged and dragged.

A large bundle full of sloshing fish was hanging in the air from the winch. A few fish slipped though the net, and a little one flopped its way towards Angie. She stretched out her arm and caught it, and she felt it dying in her palm. Gently, the fishermen pushed the bundle into the middle of the deck, untied the knots, and let the fish pour into the containers.

'*THERE'S MORE DOWN THERE*,' the captain said.

They shook the nets, rolled them up, and carried them

to the bow and onto the hauling drum. The caïque moved forward and circled again.

It was towards the end of the third and final *kaláda* that Zaramarouq was clearly visible from the deck. He was standing up, big on his lightboat, rowing amongst the waves, beast-like, roaring with seasoul laughter, shouting from out there: 'Do you like the sea, Angie? Do you like our lives, Angie?'

Angie strained to answer, but her throat was dry and her lips cracked. She went to drink water, felt disgust, spat it out. Shaky and nauseated, she glanced at the fishermen who stood above the containers, sorting out the fish: sardines with sardines, anchovies with anchovies, minnows with minnows, all into the wooden cases and on top of each case a shovelful of iodised ice. With Zaramarouq on board and the fridge full of fish, the caïque was heading off, towards the wholesale market, while the waves of the raging sea were crashing in vain.

*

Angie never felt the need to tell her one sea-story to anyone. She kept on listening with pleasure to the tales of the Egyptian fishermen at the café. She listened and learned, and learned again about their lives. But, some late nights, towards the end of her shifts at Café Papaya, when her customers had been served and she felt a little tired, Angie the waitress liked to sit behind her bar, turn her gaze towards the harbour and the sea, and think of the low and round wooden caique table with the silver soul. Then the Egyptian fishermen knew that the time had come, and they would put their beer glasses down and hush, and watch the girl with the long black hair, smiling with her eyes shut.

Acknowledgements

It was night when we were flying from Birmingham to Shanghai, and I was watching films. At some point I felt an impulse to look outside, and so I did, for the first time since we took off I looked outside, and down there I saw the lights of a night town. I glanced at the screen with the map of the airplane's route: we were flying above Kavala, my hometown.

The 24/7 café by the harbour where I had grown up working, the broken-down ice-machine, the great big sun and the customers sitting in the shade of the lemon trees, their fingers tapping on the tables, the sky that was blue and the sea that was bluer and that island opposite that was dark dark green, and that girl, the night-girl with the shadows in her eyes who wanted her cappuccino with lots of sprinkles, all those small, chipped, round trays, and the other tray, the massive one, the tray that no-one but me could master, always propped against the wobbling stool of my waitering days and nights from where I saw it all—everything might still be there.

I returned to watch the end of the film, then went for a piss.

ALEXANDROS PLASATIS is an immigrant ethnographer who writes fiction in English, his second language. His work has appeared in US, UK, Indian and Canadian magazines and anthologies. Stories from this book have been nominated for the Pushcart Prize and Best of The Net. He lives in the UK and works with displaced and vulnerable people. This is his first book.

www.alexandrosplasatis.com